I0575625

An Heir of Shadows Series

Found

By M. Stanley

© 2025 Stanley Publishing

ISBN: 979-8-9932120-0-5 (Hardcover)
ISBN: 979-8-9932120-1-2 (Paperback)
ISBN: 979-8-9932120-2-9 (E-Book)

This book is a work of fiction. Any historical figures, locations and other mentioned items are used fictitiously. All characters, events and descriptions are that of the author's imagination.

I dedicate this book to my mother. Thank you for the incredible positivity during this journey and all the feedback you provided.

<u>One</u>

Transylvania 1517

The screaming was so loud. She could hear the cries for help from miles away as she desperately flew as fast as she could to try and save her family. And yet, her wings couldn't carry her fast enough. Before her home came into view, the cries slowly drifted away. The only thing she could hear at this point was the crackling of the flames as her home burned.

And just like that, Wilhelmina Latislauve had become an orphan. She lost her family, her friends, and even her beloved. When the flames died down, Wilhelmina made her way closer to the wreckage to see if there was anything left. A memory, a family member she could lay to rest, a piece of clothing. Nothing. There was nothing left behind.

As she walked through the rubble, Wilhelmina heard a faint familiar whisper call after her, yet there was no one there.

BEEP BEEP BEEP
Chicago, IL - present day

"Stupid clock" Wilhelmina- or Mina, as she prefers - said as she was brought back to reality. Although she wouldn't complain too much, seeing how her subconscious continuously took her back to a day she wished to forget.

Mina checked the time on her clock and slowly dragged herself from her bed and headed to the bathroom. Her small, one bedroom apartment was all she needed. No one else, no pets, no friends. She was 100% on her own. She began her morning just like any other. Bathroom, breakfast, shower, teeth, get dressed. Nothing extra. She has no use for the unnecessarily extensive "get ready" routines she had seen in videos.

Mina had done many things in her life, including earning a college degree. With a certification in Polysomnography, she could work the night shift and not have to worry about going into the daylight. She had an excellent excuse if someone was to question her nocturnal schedule.

As Mina was continuing her typical routine, her phone began to vibrate on her nightstand. She walked over and unplugged it from the charger and answered, "Hello?"

"Mina, hey it's Will… so I wanted to give you a heads up that we hired another tech and want you to train him," her supervisor stated from the other end.

"Yeah, that's fine. I'll be heading to the lab soon anyway."

"Great! Thanks!"

The call ended before she could pull the phone away from her ear. Mina didn't care much for meeting new people, she tried to stay as solo as possible. New people meant more questions about her past, her family and other things she didn't want to share. She had to come up with a new past every time she moved and she definitely didn't want to talk about her family. So less people meant less questions and less room for the truth slipping out.

Mina threw on her fresh black scrubs and slid on her pink tennis shoes. She quickly grabbed something of the frozen breakfast variety from the freezer and threw it in her bag. She locked up her apartment and headed off to work. Without having far to go, seeing as she only lived a few blocks away from the lab, Mina took in the night scenery around her.

Glancing up into the night sky, Mina groaned as she saw the big nightlight in the sky, "Great," she said to herself, almost under her breath. Anyone working in the healthcare field knows all about the dreaded "full moon" shift. Even though in her line of work she only deals with one to two people a night, things can still go incredibly wrong.

She entered the building and immediately got to work by making beds and setting up equipment. She actually liked what she did, simple yet enough challenge to not bore her.

"Hey!...... Hello?" the new hire called once he entered the building.

"I'm back here, one sec!" replied Mina. As she rounded the corner she saw him. Not half bad looking but definitely not on her radar. "You can put your things there and I can show you how we arrive patients and the paperwork we go over with them once they arrive".

"Ok, sounds good. My name is Ryan by the way." He introduced himself and extended a hand for greeting.

Mina did reciprocate the handshake but replied back "Nice to meet you" she lied, "I'm Mina"

"Mina? That's an interesting name. You don't hear that one too often."

"Yea, I hear that alot" she replied, everyone always asks about her name and she always avoids providing an explanation.

The two exchanged a few personal facts about themselves with each other. Mina learned that Ryan has been a tech for about a year and lives with his parents until he can afford to move out. Mina shared she has been a tech for a while and enjoys her work.

As the night continued, Mina gave Ryan details of how the business is supposed to be run, how reports are to be generated and sent to the Doctors. All the ins and outs of the sleep lab.

Thankfully, even with it being a full moon, there wasn't anything out-of-the-norm that happened during her shift. Ryan was super helpful and a quick learner.

When the night came to an end it was 6:30am. As they were about to part ways, Ryan extended his hand to say goodbye and thank her for helping him. Mina just replied with a "you're welcome" and left to go home.

'Home' she shivered as she thought about the word. Nothing for her has been a home for over 500 years. Not since…. that day.

She doesn't mean to come off so recluse to those she meets, especially humans. But she isn't very fond of getting to know someone and then having to say goodbye when it comes time for her to move. If she stayed too long in one place then people would start to see that she doesn't age.

A severe headache began to set in and a burn in her throat arose as she made her way back to her apartment. She was hungry. The nice thing about living in Chicago was that most crime was expected and no one would really look into someone missing unless they were well known. She typically sought after the homeless, criminals, or even the blood bank if she got lucky.

Tonight took a favorable turn when she passed by an alley where a man was currently digging through a handbag that didn't seem to belong to him.

"Dammit!" the thief said in frustration. Mina watched from afar as he looked up occasionally to see if he was being watched. Once he was finished rummaging through the purse, he tossed the thing into a nearby dumpster and began walking out of the alley, completely unaware that he would not be making it home that night. Mina launched herself towards the man and latched her long sharp fangs into his neck. The man had no time to react as she pulled the life from his veins. After a minute or so, Mina pulled herself from the man and let his limp body fall to the ground. Grabbing him by the arms, she dragged him to the side and pushed him up against the wall of a building. Mina was basically a professional hunter after her many years of practice in survival mode. The people she seeks almost never see her coming unless she wants them to.

Once she got her fill, she continued on to her apartment. She had to make sure she got home in time before that ridiculous bright ball in the sky became visible. Although, she wouldn't burn and it wouldn't kill her, yet it would come with a degree of pain that she would try and avoid if she could.

Most of the vampire race would burst into a personal bon fire if caught out in the day. But not Mina. She had a special gene that was passed down to her by her grandfather. A gene that came with other benefits and skills that no other vampire would contain.

Once Mina arrived at her home, she discovered a letter at her doorstep, which partially made sense because she had no mailbox to place a letter in. Having no mailing address helped keep her untraceable. The only thing she had that could have some kind of traceability to it was a credit card she obtained a while back when she could use false information to apply.

"What the…." she stated, bending over to pick up the clean crisp envelope with it addressed to "Wilhelmina". No one had called her that since she was a young girl living in Transylvania.

She went into her apartment and opened up the envelope. Inside was a note;

Dear Wilhelmina,

Please meet us at 105 Gilberte Park at 9pm. Come alone.

Sincerely yours, The Council

"Yeah, I don't think so" she stated as she threw the letter into the waste bin that sat next to her kitchen island.

Brushing off the random note, she continued on into her bedroom and took off her tennis shoes, black scrubs, bra and panties and got into the shower. The hot steam whirling around in her bathroom was that of relaxation. A place where she could think peacefully and forget the outside world for a bit.

She continued cleaning herself with her bottle of Bath and Body Works and let the hot water roll over her. She ended her shower and dried off with a fresh, clean, fluffy white towel and threw her hair up in a second towel.

Getting ready for bed was simple, she always wore a t-shirt and shorts. She drew back her large, fluffy white comforter and slipped into silk olive green sheets.

It didn't take long for her to drift off into sleep, yet after what seemed like a minute, her eyes flew open and she popped up in her bed. "Shit!" she said "No No No! That's not possible!" her subconscious had decided to help her remember something that made the note seem more alarming now and something deserving of her full attention.

<u>Two</u>

"The Council? No, that can't be right." She began pacing again around her room. "This doesn't make sense. How would they have found me now? How could they even still be around?"

The Council was a group consisting of three old men put together by her father to create the laws within the vampire race. Or rather, to document and uphold the laws her father created. She figured they had just perished at the time when everyone else did.

Without hesitation, she began grabbing the important things. There was no time to properly pack. Although she typically spent twenty to twenty five years in a place before moving on, and it had only been about ten years since she had moved to Chicago, the note meant the Council had survived all those years and somehow found her.

Trying not to spend too much time thinking about the note, Mina focused on getting out of there. Abruptly, she came to a halt with her rushed packing and realised that she couldn't leave yet. She was stuck to the surrounding walls of her home for at least another four hours.

"Stupid sun" she expressed. Although she did contemplate the idea of just risking it and getting out of there. But she took a deep breath and allowed herself to slow down and wait for the sun to set.

While she waited, she wrote out a note for her landlord and left an extra month's rent on her counter. Her landlord always treated her with kindness and never disturbed her during the day, even though he never really reached out to her at all. Her topsy turvy sleep schedule reminded her that she also had to let her employer know that she was no longer able to continue her employment with them, effective immediately.

As the time passed, she looked out her window from the living room and saw that the sun had set enough for her to make a move.

Before walking out the front door to leave another chapter behind, she took one more second to look back at her little apartment. She then closed the door and placed the key under the mat.

Walking through the city to the train station, she was on high alert but made sure not to seem like she was in a rush. The last thing she needed was for someone to ask if she was alright or to draw attention to herself. She bought a train ticket to head south, and continued to the platform. She had no idea when she would get off, but she just had to start going in some kind of direction. Once on the train, she could figure out the specifics a little better.

As she was about to board the train, a feeling came over her as if she were being followed. Although familiar, it was something she had not felt in a long time. She looked around yet saw no one recognizable, so she boarded the train quickly and found her seat. She pulled out her phone to look at the train's route to see what may be her destination, 'North Carolina may be nice, or maybe Charleston,' she thought to herself. Both were sunny and she could easily get into another sleep lab if needed. She hadn't been to either place in over a hundred years, so there would be no risk in someone remembering her.

As the train began to move, she heard that same whisper from her dream. This time, she was awake.

****

Transylvania - present day

"We need to find her," stated Radu. "She is the last living monarch of the race. Our people need leadership!" The Council was made up of three men, Radu, Gregor, and Vasile. They were not vampires, but they also could not die. All who stayed in Transylvania after the fall of their king, refusing to travel away from their home. They enjoyed their solitude, except for when their maid came to clean and such.

The Council sat together at a large table which had multiple pictures laid out of the missing princess, her last known whereabouts, her activities, etc. Yet not one of them had any idea of how to get her back, or how to convince her to return and take the throne for the vampire race. There weren't many left who survived the attack, but there were enough and they needed a ruler. Many of the older vampires still residing in the region stayed true to tradition and wanted the monarchy back. The humans had a democracy, but the vampires wanted what they had once before.

"We don't have much time before her subjects start to move on and decide they no longer want to be ruled by a monarchy", said Gregor with haste in his voice.

As two of the Council members bounced back and forth,discussing the reasons for finding their princess, the third was sitting at a secluded desk off to the side of the room by a window. Vasile was reading through one of the last laws they had recorded before the passing of their beloved king. Double checking that getting the lost princess back was best for the race and to make sure it was in fact legal to bring her back, even if it was against her will.

"We shouldn't do any talking! Just hire someone to find her and bring her back. No questions asked", said Radu.

"We cannot do that," said Vasile by the window, "The king's law clearly states that no one can be forced to take the throne unless immediate danger is present. Currently, there is no danger, just an empty throne. The princess has every right to decline her right. The monarchy would end and someone would have to be voted in. She just gets first say".

"But Vasile, we know for a fact that she won't take the throne. So it must be placed upon her", said Gregor, "everyone figured the lost princess was still alive and since then they have held out hope for her return to rule. There could be a riot on our hands if she refuses"

"It is a discussion that must happen if we are to respect the king's law" said Vasile.

The three men discussed things further, attempting to find loopholes in the king's law that would help them.

"We will confront her and explain to her what needs to happen. It is time she accepts her status and takes over the race as she was born to do. There is no other capable heir." said Gregor.

The old men conversed some more and came to an agreement. They must find princess Wilhelmina and bring her back to Transylvania to rule the race. But who could they get to bring her back? That was a discussion for another day as the three men decided it was time to eat and then retire to their rooms.

Little did they know that finding the princess would be the easiest part of getting her back to the throne.

Three

Transylvania 1509

"I'm not sure why I have to be at the ball, it's not like I'm the one who must find a male and marry right away." said Wilhelmina, youngest of three daughters.

"My dear, it is a ball in honor of your 16th birthday. You should be excited about coming out to society." stated Eliahna, maid to the three princesses of the race.

Wilhelmina was 15 years old and had no reason to come out to a society she wanted no part of. She very much disliked Court and loathed the idea of being married to a man who didn't see her as an equal. She often spent most of her time reading, writing, or in some instances, flying. Yes, Wilhelmina had wings. She was the only one in her family to have them, and only her mother and maid knew about it.

Wilhelmina's grandfather was none other than Vladimir II Dracul himself, otherwise known as Dracula. Wilhelmina carried the same gene that her grandfather had; a gene that was passed down to one person, every other generation. Her sisters didn't get it, but for some reason, fate chose her. She loved it though. She loved soaring through the sky early in the morning before the sun was about to rise.

The queen of the race, Queen Khaterina, entered the girls' bed chamber. Their mother had a beauty about her that was unmatched. She was graceful with every move she made and had the sweetest voice of anyone in the race. Many say that the youngest princess will carry on her mothers beauty when she is fully matured at age 21.

"Wilhelmina, you haven't chosen a dress yet for your ball?" her mother asked, "I believe the red gown would be most appropriate for you. To represent the fire in your heart and the wild in your eyes."

"But mother, I wanted to wear the red dress. Lord Cristian's favorite color is red and I'd like to impress him." came a comment from the eldest daughter, Natahlia. The first born princess was also born of beauty, class and a willingness to do as was needed of her. In this case, being the first to wed.

"Be careful, Nataliah, you wouldn't want to seem too eager for Lord Cristian. He may deem you a bit over interested and run away" poked Wilhelmina.

Her eldest sister began to make a move to punish Wilhelmina for the snide comment, but was stopped by their queen mother.

"Wilhelmina decides first and I personally believe the red will look best on her" replied their mother.

"I'd say you are right mother, I, too, believe I would look best in the red," said Wilhelmina, which came with a slight smirk to her oldest sister.

"As long as I get the blue dress, that is all I care about" came the middle sister, Ana, who was sitting at her vanity. Ana made sure she always looked her best. She had the eye of many suitors and never wanted to disappoint.

"I'll make this simple for all of you girls" came their mother, "Nataliah, you wear the gold. Ana, wear the blue. And Wilhelmina will be in red."

As their mother showed herself out, Elianah walked over to the window where Wilhelmina was sitting. Leaning in to look out the window, as if to gaze at what the princess was staring at, she made a quiet statement, "If you go now, you will be in your chambers before sunrise." Wilhelmina's face lit up with life and she bolted out of her bed chamber. She swiftly made her way down the stone corridor of the castle and down a winding stairway that conveniently led

*down to the horse stable. The stable was a place where
Mina could leave as if going for a ride but it was to go to
the woods and spread her wings. Once she entered through
the wooded double door entrance, her second reason for
loving the stable walked out into her path.*

*The stable hand she had known since they were both
children greeted her just as he would greet any other
member of the royal family; with a bow and, just for
Wilhelmina, a special smile.*

*Wilhelmina replied with a smile as well while she
greeted the young man, "Dimitri"*

****

*The now 17 year old stablehand had been sold to the
king at age 9 to tend to the king's horses. He was born in
Russia and found by the king during his travels. Dimitri's
family was poor, especially since his father (a lord at the
Russian Court who had a one-time-only night with a
female) had left before Dimitri's mother knew she was
pregnant. His mother raised him the best she could, but
when the king offered to buy him, she knew he may have a
chance at a better life with the Transylvanian king. Dimitri
was only a couple years older than Mina but the romantic
interest arose as they matured.*

'Mina looks beautiful as always', Dimitri thought to himself when the princess came into the stable. He made it a point to intercept her path so he could greet her. Mostly so he could just speak to her, even if it was only for a second. Dimitri knew she was off limits due to her status, no stable boy would ever be allowed to marry a princess. But not being able to have her made him desire her even more. And he knew Mina felt the same way. "And how is the young princess this day?" he asked.

"I'm well my dear Dimitri, I am well, thank you. And you? How are things here in the stable?"

"Things are well, but my day has certainly improved now that you are here in front of me."

"Dimitri, you know I'm more than happy and willing to come see you whenever circumstances allow."

"Yes, your highness, of course.", he replied. "And how might I be of service?" with a slight lift in the corner of his smile, knowing the princess picked up exactly how he felt towards her. Mina was not the type of princess to tell her father the stable hand was being inappropriate or improper towards her. No, she was much more free spirited than her sisters- or the rest of Court for that matter.

"I require a mount. I feel the need for a little adventure before the ball tomorrow. Today has held too much seriousness for my taste."

Dimitri made the sly comment under his breath, "I can be your mount".

"What was that?"

"Nothing princess. I'll saddle you the best mount we have in the stable. I'll be back in just a moment."

Dimitri walked away to get his princess a good mount, one who was sturdy and would not spook easily. He went up to a large white horse, whose coat had a small amount of dapple to it. The horse was large but he knew Mina would not be intimidated by him, so he tacked up the horse with a freshly cleaned saddle and bridle and checked his hooves. "Fresh shoes, good." he said quietly to himself, no reason to risk the horse losing a shoe and possibly hurting the princess in the process. Dimitri led the horse over to his female, uh, his princess.

"Here we are, your mount my princess. I made sure his girth is tight and his hooves have good shoes so nothing will interfere with your ride.", Dimitri said.

"Ah, thank you", the princess stated while seeming slightly distracted with her own thoughts. "Dimitri", she said as he began walking away to tend to his chores, " If I told you something, about a personal matter, would you hear my words?" Taken by her words, Dimitri kept silent.

She added in the awkward silence, "In a sense that, it was pertaining to......"

Dimitri continued looking at her, curious as she hesitated in her sentence.

"To what my princess?" He said eagerly, assuming he already knows what she was about to say. Hoping it was something pertaining to their feelings for one another.

"You." She abruptly said. Her answer had opened the door to a certain conversation that needed to be had. Dimitri had always wanted to confess his love to the princess, and now he felt he may have his chance.

"It would be my pleasure to hear what you have to say, your highness. About anything, I'm yours to listen or anything else you require.", he replied with a grin on his face which showed satisfaction in knowing the princess was in fact, his.

Neither of the young vampires had ever been in this situation before and had no idea how to navigate the restless waters called love. Dimitri knew how he felt and held hope that she felt the same. Only time would tell if this was a match meant to last.

As they both were silent in their moment of 'deeper conversation', from the shadows emerged a tall male figure with a look of aggression on his face. Dragos.

Things had to become serious quickly before the king's hand had any thought that he and the princess were doing anything other than speaking of the horse. Mina was the first to speak, "Thank you Dimitri, I appreciate your swiftness in collecting and readying my mount. I shall return in one hour. My mount shall require fresh water and hay when we return."

"Yes, your highness. Please remember that the sun is set to rise in the next two hours", Dimitri replied, all business in his voice and seriousness on his face.

"Yes, of course", Mina replied.

As the princess walked out of the barn, she threw the leather reins over the horse's head and mounted it. She took off at a gallop through the open land and headed towards the woods.

Once the princess was out of sight, Dimitri turned back towards the hand and said "Is there something I may help you with sir? I can provide you a mount as well if you wish to accompany the princess."

Before replying to the young boy, Dragos gave him a serious look over. Dimitri could tell that Dragos was trying to read him and see if there was anything he was hiding.

"No" he finally said, "I don't require a mount, but you had better mind how you speak to the princess. Is she worth losing not only your job, but your life?"

Dimitri thought of what he said and then spoke, "I respect the royal family and would risk my life for any of them", 'but only Mina', he thought to himself.

"Well I'm sure they all appreciate your loyalty. But hear what I say boy: stay in your place and do not speak

out of turn." said Dragos coldly, as if he knew what was actually occurring.

"Yes, sir, of course."

"Carry on then."

"Yes, sir."

As Dragos took his leave, Dimitri felt he could finally breathe. He turned around to look out the double door entry/exit of the stable where the princess galloped from. All he could think about was what she wanted to speak to him about. That item between his legs began to pulsate with just the mere thought of her. The way her hips were moving in the saddle while she rode her horse to the woods. God, what he would give to see her without that barrier of clothing she wore. But her coming out ball was tomorrow and he knew that once that happened, she was on the market for being matched with someone higher up in social status.

"I'll see you soon, my princess." Dimitri stated before returning to his chores.

<u>Four</u>

"Now arriving in Savannah, Georgia!" the overhead announcement proclaimed.

Mina had slept for the majority of her trip and decided when she woke up, wherever she was, was going to be her home for the next twenty or so years, unless any other interruptions interfered with her plans.

Mina gathered her belongings and got off the train. Thankfully, she didn't have much to fuss with, only a duffle bag and her purse. Looking around she could remember being here in the 1920's. Of course, a lot had changed since then, but she could remember the long parties and her social status. At that time she was seeing a gentleman who was somewhat wealthy and found an undeniable pleasure in showing her off. Although she didn't mind the wild nights that lifestyle brought, it did create more work for her to disappear without reason and possibly at a moment's notice. She always had to create a valid reason for leaving or commit some kind of crime to be taken away to ensure others did not look for her. She didn't mind though, nothing scared her and she couldn't be harmed. Definitely not by any human that is, and any vampire who attempted it was unsuccessful.

It was about 7am when she arrived in Georgia and, thankfully for her, it was a perfectly cloudy day. Yes, there would still be UV rays coming through the clouds but it wasn't pure sunlight. Mina began walking down the platform where her train was, taking a left down a hall and down some steps that led to a parking lot. Being in a new place meant she needed to create a new profile for herself. Once she gets to some kind of housing, she will sit down with a nice glass of wine and rehearse what she will tell people if they ask. If she has anything to do with it she will try and avoid that possible scenario altogether.

Mina found a bench and set her things down on it before taking a seat herself. She pulled out her phone and began to look into housing. Something that didn't require a background check and something that she could get into quickly.

While scrolling through multiple listings in the area, she came across an ad for a beautiful small farmhouse just on the outskirts of Savannah.

"Perfect" she stated to herself.

Looking further into the ad, she saw that the person was just hoping someone in need could use it and they rent out on the 'honors' system. Meaning they collected rent by a check in their mailbox and as long as they met you, there weren't any background checks. Everything was based on just a good old fashioned verbal agreement and a handshake. Other than that, you were left completely alone.

Entering the phone number with the pad of her finger, she called and spoke to the sweet elderly woman who answered. Her name was June and she had owned the home since her father passed away just a month ago and just decided to post it. June stated to Mina that she'd like to meet in person around 10am today to give her a tour and get an idea of who Mina was. Mina agreed, hung up the phone and looked at the time. '7:30am' was displayed on her phone's lock screen.

"Excuse me, is there anyone sitting with you? I'm waiting for my ride and nowhere else is available to sit and wait". Mina looked up from her phone and saw an elderly gentleman standing with nothing but a briefcase and a newspaper. He was dressed in a suit and looked like he was heading to the office.

"Oh, no one." Mina moved her things out of the man's way so he had room to sit. "Thank you," he said. "Are you coming home or waiting for a train?" the man asked.

"Coming. I have a new job opportunity coming my way and chose to move closer so I could be available if they needed me in person", guess she found her new story.

"Oh really? What's the job? I know some of the businesses around here, perhaps im familiar with it"

'Shit', she thought to herself, and answered " it's called I.A.A.V. LLC. It's a new start up and I work for the HR side of it. I'm mostly working from home right now". She slightly giggled to herself (I.A.A.V. - I Am A Vampire).

"Oh! No, unfortunately I haven't heard of that company. Well, I hope you like Savannah. It's a good old city, lots of history". The man looked up and saw that a black car with tinted windows had pulled up. A driver in a suit came around from the driver's side and opened the door for him.

"Need a ride? The kind man asked her.

"No thank you, I'm waiting for a friend to get me", she lied.

"Well, you have a great day then. And welcome to Savannah!" The man smiled at Mina as he slowly got into the car. The driver shut his door and walked swiftly to the other side where he got in and drove the kind man away.

Mina thought to herself that maybe she should have accepted the ride, but that would mean more conversation she wasn't willing to have.

An hour passed by and she decided the bench at the
train station had spent enough time with her ass and
decided she should start making her way to her meeting
with June.

Even though Mina was around for most of the United
States history, she still loved visiting the old cities that have
seen as much as she has. It was like coming back to a
friend.

She started walking in the direction of the farmhouse
as she followed the GPS on her phone. The farmhouse was
only about 6 miles from where she was, but far enough
from the city that you couldn't hear its noise. She walked
alone for a while until she started seeing wide open fields.
Mina began having small flashbacks to her past again,
flying in the night sky, back when she was actually
enjoying her life. Perhaps this new home will allow her to
spread her wings and be a little more free than she had been
recently.

As she walked and had a nice trip down memory lane
(for once), she started getting that feeling that someone
familiar was near once again. She would look around but
not see anyone. No cars, no one else walking, not even any
animals. She heard the whisper again, 'Mina'.

Stopping dead in her tracks, she took a good look
around. Still no one.

"Who are you?!" Mina yelled out, somehow expecting a reply to be reciprocated.

With there being no answer, she began walking again, but this time on full alert. She could hear cars and people far away from her and even heard some cows chewing the thick green grass that was in a pasture a mile back or so. Yet…. no voice.

Mina arrived at her potential new home and goodness, was it adorable. The farmhouse was all white, including the shutters, and had a porch the length of the house. There was a small shed to the right that butted up to the tree line and a few trees in the front yard.

Admiring the simplicity of the old home, Mina walked up the short driveway to the front door and knocked. An elderly woman meandered to the front door and opened it wide for her.

"Welcome! Gosh, you are a beautiful young lady aren't you?" June said. Young? Mina was at least 5 times the woman's age but welcomed the compliment.

"Thank you, you have a beautiful home by the way. I assume it was built in the 19th century?" Mina replied

"Why, yes, it was! Are you familiar with older homes?"

"To a degree, I've always liked looking at old houses. I suppose I just adopted a talent for guessing their age"

"Well, as long as you don't try and guess my age deary."

Mina thought about it and considered the woman's fraile heart rhythm, the thickness of her glasses and how short her breath was just from walking a few steps. She'd say late 80's early 90's.

"I wouldn't dare, but I'd say not a day over 40."

"Well aren't you a sweet one. I feel as though you will work out just fine as my new tenant."

The woman continued on with the tour. Upstairs there was a bedroom and a bathroom equipped with a tub and sink.The second bedroom was downstairs. The kitchen was also small but fully functional for one person and included a small eating area in the far corner. The living room came right off the kitchen and included a large collection of books that were placed neatly on an old bookshelf. Finally, they went down to the unfinished basement where the washer and dryer resided.

"Well, everything seems perfect. Would I be able to move in today?"

"Of course. Rent is due the first of every month. You can just write me a check or leave cash in an envelope inside my mailbox. I live just up the road, the small red cottage with enough flowers surrounding it to support a spring wedding."

"Sounds perfect", Mina replied, "I don't have a lot of stuff, but I'll drop off my first rent payment tomorrow night, if that's alright. I work third shift on my computer and won't be awake until night".

"Oh, that's fine dear. You just call me or pop over anytime if you need anything. And feel free to use anything inside the home you may need." June left Mina with her new house key and showed herself out.

"Here's to another new beginning", proclaimed Mina as she stood in the entryway between the living room and the door to the basement. She took the wooden stairs up to one of the bedrooms that faced the road and began to put her clothes away. Thankfully the place came furnished, so she didn't have to worry much about ordering furniture.

'Mina' came the whisper.

Mina looked around once more as if the whisper came from directly behind her. Still no one to be seen. Was she being haunted? Why did this whisper just now begin?

She was unsure of the details but one thing was for certain.

The voice was getting closer.

<u>Five</u>

Mina rolled over in her bed and looked at her phone. '8pm' her phone clock displayed. Mina had fallen asleep after she had unpacked her things and placed them in the appropriate places. Due to her travel day, her typical daily routine had been thrown off. When she awoke, she had pushed back the quilt that was placed on the bed before her arrival and replaced it after her feet hit the hardwood floor.

Mina found the light switch on the wall and the light illuminated the room. She walked over to the window to take a look outside to see if there was anything to be seen, but there was nothing. Nothing for miles around; she was completely alone.

She turned on a few lights and walked down the wooden stairs to the kitchen. The one thing she didn't think to get before turning in for the day was food. She wasn't ready to go out and hunt just yet, not until she got a lay of

the land and knew for sure there weren't going to be any
surprises.

Mina decided it was as good a time as any to go ahead
and take a walk around the property. Walking back upstairs,
she shifted her clothes around until she found what she was
looking for. Mina took some black leggings and a gray
t-shirt and got ready. She never felt the need to get dressed
up, and never made an effort to try and impress others.
Mina found some socks to add to her outfit and went back
downstairs.

Once she reached the first floor, she found her tennis
shoes and walked out the back door, which was placed
directly in line with the front door. After she closed the
door, Mina turned towards the field and just looked out into
the vast space of green grass. Verifying that she couldn't
hear or see anything besides wildlife, she began to walk
around the perimeter of the property.

Having great eyesight was one thing, but having night
vision was even better. Being a natural predator gave her
that ability, so she didn't need any additional light to help
her see in pure darkness, with or without the moon. Stealth
was her best trait, next to immortality.

Continuing through the field, Mina still wasn't finding
any evidence of another person. Human or vampire. She
saw some deer, heard a running stream and picked up on
some cows mooing a mile or so down the road. Still,

nothing close to her. Choosing to try and hunt, she walked back to where she had seen the group of deer. Animal blood was acceptable but didn't hold her over like human blood. Like having a veggie burger instead of a real burger, filling but not satisfying.

There they were, a small group of deer were minding their own business and grazing in the plush green field. One happened to shoot its head straight up as if it knew it were being hunted. Not seeing anything, it lowered its head and continued on with the grass.

Mina slowly, without making a sound, moved closer to the group. She could hear their hearts beginning to race and the blood pumping through their veins.

Allowing her sharp white fangs to descend, she gave into her animalistic instincts and attacked. There was no way for the deer to see her coming as she launched off her feet and was on one of the deer before it could look up. Of course, the others made a break for it and scattered to avoid being on the meal card as well. Pulling and sucking on the animal's vein, Mina got what she needed. She loathed feeding on animals due to the unnecessary hair that was stuck to her when she was finished.

Picking up the limp body she had just used as a personal juice box, she took the deer to the edge of the woods where some other animal could enjoy the rest of her kill.

Crack

Mina whipped her head around and got low to the ground, someone was coming. Or something,

Voices. She began to hear voices on the other side of the field. Not human.

Sniffing the air to pick up a scent, she determined there were two men - males- walking towards her.

'Other vampires? Here?', she questioned in her head.

Confused, she stood up to confront the pair and see what warranted them coming onto the property. There was no nervousness in her because she was not scared or worried that something would happen to her. It was the males who should be scared.

****

Sam and Dom decided to leave their campsite and go out looking for food. They hadn't fed in a couple days, so they were definitely on the hunt for something large.

As they exited the woods, a mile or two from where their camp was located, they entered a large field. They continued walking, when they stopped abruptly. Out on the other side of the field, they saw what looked like a woman, bent over, holding something. She stood up and walked with something large draped over her shoulder.

'Was that a deer?' Sam thought to himself. As she dropped the load, the two males decided to confront her.

Gaining ground, they came closer and closer, not paying much attention to where they stepped. Then Dom, the big foot, stepped on a stick on the ground and seemingly spooked the female. She whipped her head around towards them and flashed her fangs, a sign of warning.

****

"Can I help you?" Mina asked, not caring which one was to answer her first.

"Nope, just passing through. Nice kill by the way. With the deer. Not your first time hunting, huh?" said the taller of the two. He seemed young but you could never tell how old he really was. He had jet black hair that was cut short and clothes that seemed like they hadn't been washed in a while.

"No. Not my first kill", replied Mina, "what are you doing on this property?"

"Like I said, no reason, just taking a walk to maybe find something to eat. What are you doing here?"

"I live here, I'm renting the house that resides on this property."

"Oh, nice, glad to see someone is finally living there" the male stated.

'Okay, enough of this back and forth that is seeming to become a conversation', Mina thought to herself. Before she could speak up and end the chit chat, the tall male spoke, "What's your name? I'm Sam and this is Dominic, or Dom is what we call him"

Not really caring much for the introductions, Mina gave a brief smile and walked away.

"Hey, wait!" The one named Sam reached out and grabbed Mina by the arm.

Big. Mistake.

Mina grabbed the young male by the throat with her free hand and squeezed, hard enough where the male collapsed to his knees immediately.

"Do not touch me" she stated sharply.

With a raspy voice, due to his restricted airway, the male stated "Okay, I'm sorry. Let..... Me..... go."

With that Mina released him from her vice grip and began to walk again. That's when the other male, Dom, decided to make a move to defend his friend. The second male was shorter and a little heavier than the other. He had short brown hair and seemed a little clumsy. Mina heard

every movement he made and could play out what he was
doing in her head without even having to see him.

At the perfect timing, she stepped to the right and the
male stumbled. Quickly getting to his feet, he tried his
attack again, this time from head on.

As he came towards her, she grounded herself and
lunged at he male. Meeting each other halfway, Mina
placed her arm around his neck, flipped him to his back and
stood over him while she lowered herself down and placed
her knees on his biceps.

"You young ones don't learn. Do you?" she said with a
stern yet cocky look.

"Who are you?" Sam asked, watching from a few
paces away as his friend was dominated.

"My name isn't important. What is important is that
you know your place and do not come through or near here
again. I prefer my solitude and if anyone were to interrupt
it, there would be a price to pay."

"You got it" Dom said quickly, trying to tap out on
Mina's leg so she would remove her weight from him.

Mina stood up and allowed the two to leave.

As she watched the two pretty much run away from
her, she chose to head back to the house. No television, no
entertainment of any kind. She pulled out her phone and
began scrolling the internet. With nothing much to read
about that caught her attention, she went to the dusty

bookshelf and found a book that might contain something interesting to keep her mind busy. She always loved to read, and could do so anywhere, anytime. She read the book for an hour or so, but was interrupted when she picked up the sound of footsteps approaching her back porch.

Knock knock knock

'Who could that be?', She thought to herself, as she pulled out her phone to check the time '12am'. She took a listen to have some kind of heads up as to who her mysterious visitor may be. Definitely not human, so there was a good chance it was another vampire.

Placing the book down without keeping the page she was on, she stood up from the couch and walked over to the back door.

It was the two young males from before. This time accompanied by a slightly larger group who were probably wanting to see who the female was that supplied the aggression towards the boys.

Mina stepped out and the taller one, Sam? Was it?, spoke first.

"We need to talk."

<u>Six</u>

Transylvania 1509

As the princess, Mina had certain duties that she must perform and standards that she must uphold. But not right now. Not in this moment where it was just her and her mount, whom she secured to a tree with enough slack in the rein to allow him to graze while waiting for her to return.

Mina looked around once more to check she wasn't followed and would not be seen. She removed her gown, so as not to dirty it, and placed it neatly by a tree. Above the top of her corset, her bare back had what seemed like bruising, yet was in a particular pattern. Almost like a faint tattoo of wings that had been on her back since she was six.

Relaxing her mind, she freed her wings from the flesh of her back and admired them. Her wings were that of immaculate beauty as they were pure black and full as the

*wings of an angel. Walking to the edge of the clearing
where she had secured her mount, she began running
towards the other side and as she reached the other edge
she gave herself flight. Her wings were pumping as she
gained more and more height. She soared through the night
sky and admired the stars as she felt she could reach up to
them to touch them.*

Free.

*She always felt like nothing in the world mattered
anymore when she was as flying free as a bird. Although
she never stayed up for long, just so she did not risk being
seen.*

*After a while she lowered herself back down to ground
and relaxed her wings back into their fleshy prison. Before
deciding to go back to the castle, Mina found a fallen tree
near the clearing and took a seat. She often took time to
admire the woods, how secluded things were and how she
could be herself in them. Neither the trees, nor wild
animals ever judged her for the way she was. After taking a
moment, she decided it was time to head back to the castle
before someone was sent out to find her.*

*Stepping into her gown, she pulled it up into place and
was able to re-tie the backing on her own. After enough
times, she was a pro at putting herself back together. Using
the same fallen tree, Mina mounted her horse with ease and
galloped back to the stable.*

As she dismounted, she put her gown back into place after riding astride, and pulled the reins back up over the horse's head so she could lead him into the stable. As soon as she entered the stable, a voice came from behind her.

"Did my princess have a successful ride this night?" said Dimitri

"Why yes I did. Good choice for a mount as well. He was sure footed and didn't twitch at anything along the trail", she replied to him with a slight smile on her face.

"Wonderful, it pleases me to see you return safely from your adventure. Allow me to finish taking care of your mount after a long ride."

"Thank you" she said as she handed him the reins.

As she handed him the reins, their hands brushed each other. It was like an electric shock that was more pleasure than pain.

As Dimitri walked off, she stood still watching him. His shoulder length hair was black as night, and pulled back in a piece of leather to keep it out of his face. She noticed his arms were strong under the sleeves of the white blouse he was wearing. She took in the sight of him as he took care of the mount who carried her to the clearing and back.

'What it must be like to be in those arms' she thought as Dimitri walked the horse back into its stall.

"All set, fresh water and hay for him, just as you requested", Dimitri said as he walked back over to her.

Only this time, he stood closer to her than before. Close enough that she could almost feel his heart beat pounding away. He was excited but nervous to be near her.

"I very much appreciate all you did for the horse. He is possibly the most pampered animal in the stable thanks to you", she replied with a slight quiver in her voice.

"Well I do what I can, my princess, to make sure any mount of yours is treated with the best of best."

"Is there something I can do for you? In regards to the short distance you have put between us?"

Mina hoped he would not move away, she enjoyed having him close. Was it too close for how a stable boy should be to a royal member? Yes. Did she care? No.

"Well, my princess, I had hoped we could possibly entertain that question you were wanting to ask me earlier..."

"Oh, that. Well, I, um..." She couldn't think with him being that near to her. All she could think about was how his lips must taste or how his body, hidden under all that clothing, might feel. Thoughts a princess should not be having.

But she was having them, and they could not be ignored for long, if at all.

"Might I assume what the question was and try to give you an answer?" Dimitri said as he looked down to her.

"Unless you've become a mind reader, I'm not sure you can provide a valid answer."

"Allow me to try, my princess"

After his statement, he lowered his head down to her own and placed his lips upon hers. He pulled back after he gave her a taste so he could gaze at her and see if that answered her question.

"Well? Was I correct?", he flirted.

Without wasting a moment, she reached up to his neck and pulled him back down to her. Coming together once more, yet holding the place for longer. Dimitri took her by the waist without breaking their connection and escorted her to an empty stall to attempt some privacy. Not that anyone should be coming down to the stable for another hour or so for the final check, but one could never be too careful.

Pushing her up against the cold wooden stable wall, he placed one of his arms up above her to brace himself and the other on the small of her back.

The kissing continued for a moment before Dimitri pulled back from her.

"Princess, may I continue? May I go on my own adventure tonight with you?", he questioned before continuing to make sure that's what she wanted.

"Yes.", her answer was short but to the point. She wanted this. Him. She wanted him.

Dimitri lowered his mouth back down to her and every so often slipped his tongue into her mouth as a tease. She reciprocated the action to show she was in this with him, and welcomed him to her with no protest.

****

Taking the hand that was at her back, he slowly brought it around to the front of her gown. 'Damn gowns never made it easy for one to gain entry to the other', Dimitri thought to himself as he tried to undo what he could. He wanted to see the body which was hidden beneath the multiple layers of cloth. He craved to see all of her.

Since the two had gotten older, all Dimitri could think about was being with his princess. Never knowing if she would want the same in return, he always hoped she did. This was proof, this was that dream coming true.

Dimitri never had much in life, he was sold to the vampire king when he was but 10 years old and had been working in the stable ever since. He loved horses so it wasn't very difficult to work there, plus every so often he was met with the most beautiful of the three sisters. He had loved Princess Wilhelmina since they met at that young age.

Bringing himself back to the undeniable miracle in front of him, he returned his mind to his female. Finally, yet carefully, he was able to get through the first layer of her dress. As the dress slid down, Mina was left in her undergarments, but she didn't move a muscle. 'Shit, the corset', he said in his head. He tried his best, but he could not get past the layer of fabric and whale bone that made up an article of clothing to give a female a smaller waist.

Dimitri chose to try another way to get to his princess. As his hand began to travel south, he paused as he broke their connection and looked upon her. As if they were talking with their eyes, Mina picked up on what he was wanting to do, she seemingly trusted him.

"Yes. I want you to touch me." She eagerly said and her breath ran short.

"With pleasure, my princess" he said, as he continued his adventure with her.

Dimitri reconnected his mouth with hers and used his hand to move other layers of fabric out of his way so he could feel her. His hand finally reached the point where he had access to her most sensitive part. He lifted his lips from hers and moved his head to her neck, as he began softly teasing her with his teeth and then began kissing. At the same time, he was sliding two of his fingers up and down between her legs. Feeling the wetness she produced as a sign of immense pleasure. Without any protest from her, he continued on by going deeper inside her. Exploring more of her with his hand, he heard her gasp slightly as his two fingers entered her all the way and began to enter and retreat repeatedly.

He waited for a sign of protest but there was none.

****

Mina couldn't think about anything. She was so enveloped with what Dimitri was doing that she would not stop him. Even if someone was watching, she didn't care.

The touch of Dimitri's hand between her legs was something she had never had before, but she loved it. She loved......Him.

Slowly she could feel herself getting more and more lost in the pleasure, feelings as if she was going to boil over. She wanted him to see all of her but her ridiculous dress was in the way.

All of a sudden, she felt Dimitri remove his hand that was inside her and spun her around so she was facing away from him. She looked at him in confusion, thinking that he may not want to look at her for the remainder of their little adventure.

He noticed this and reassured her, "It's alright my princess, trust me."

She did. She allowed him to do what he was set to do. She could feel him pulling at her and next thing she knew, she could breathe a little easier. Her lungs were able to expand to their full capacity as her corset was loosened. Dimitri had loosened it just enough to show what he sought after but could easily pull it back into place if someone happened to come down.

She was turned back around and stood there as he took in the sight of her.

Her breasts were sized to her body with perfection and she watched him take his hand and run it along the top of her collar bone. Slowly, he traced the middle of her sternum down to her left breast and grabbed ahold of it. She felt the warmth of his hand upon her and let him explore her more.

Being turned around again, he was directly behind her. Lowering his head back to the side of her neck, he wrapped one arm around her and the other was placed onto her breast. He massaged the plush skin and played with her nipple while taking it between his fingers and rolling it around. Mina was beside herself as he teased her more and more, unsure of how much more she could take before she would explode. The stable felt so hot, she wondered how it hadn't caught fire yet.

She was about to tell Dimitri to take her, when all of a sudden she could hear someone asking for her from 2 floors above.

"Stop. We must.... stop. Someone is coming for me", she declared as she turned around to face him. She didn't want to push him away but for his own safety and her virtue, she had to get dressed. He helped her with the corset as she started pulling up her gown. Tying the back up on her own as she did many times before, she and Dimitri reemerged from the empty stall. Her cheeks still felt hot and could tell she had to clean herself up due to the pleasure from below.

"Someone is coming," she whispered.

Mutually, they began a conversation about the weather and the horses. He was telling her that once the final check was complete, they would turn the horse out to pasture for the day so they could enjoy the sun.

The heavy footfalls determined who it was that was coming to find her. Dragos. Of course, her father would send down that beast to retrieve her.

"Princess," he said with a bow. "Your father is wondering why you are not in your chambers yet. The sun will be out soon and he requests that you do not risk being exposed."

"Yes, I was just on my way up. Dimitri here was explaining to me how the stable is run after we are all

inside for the day." Mina replied, not letting anything on that they were up to something completely inappropriate.

"I understand. I was told to escort you to your bed chambers"

"Yes, thank you" Turning to Dimitri, she said, "Thank you for your assistance with my mount and taking such good care of the others in the stable. We all appreciate your work here."

"You're welcome, your highness," Dimitri replied with a bow of his own.

Mina walked off with the beast and wanted to turn to look at Dimitri one more time before going back inside, but she didn't risk it. She continued to follow Dragos up the steps to the floor where her chambers were and found Elihana was waiting for her. Elihana always took care of the daughters before bed, helped them dress and such, and made sure everything was in order before turning in for the day.

"Did you have a good ride?" Elihana asked Mina.

"I did, it was a beautiful morning for a ride before turning in for bed" Mina replied.

She undressed and her maid took the gown away and helped Mina into her night dress. Mina knew she still needed to handle one more thing before falling asleep, but not until Elihana was gone. Mina climbed into her bed and got comfortable as Elihana came over and wished her goodnight. The maid showed herself out and closed up the bed chambers.

Mina immediately rose from her bed and found a cloth she would use to dry off with after her bath, did what was needed and threw it to the side where other dirty linens were kept. Mina quickly ran back to her bed and was fast asleep in no time with a large smile across her face. She would dream of her future with Dimitri and of her father being accepting of them together.

Little did she know, her dreams would never come true.

<u>Seven</u>

Mina stood in the doorway at the back of the house with her arms folded tight against her. Seemingly annoyed that these two males had not gotten the hint from earlier that she did not want visitors, and yet, they brought company.

"My earlier warning when I pinned your friend there to the ground was to tell you to get lost and not come back. So explain to me why you're standing here on my doorstep", Mina asked with a stern irritated tone.

"These are my family, in a sense. We were asked when we got back what had happened and when they heard we were confronted by a 'new in town' vampire, they wanted to meet you" Sam said.

"Do you fully understand that I'm not the one to be tested? I don't want to meet your family, I have no interest in finding friends"

"Then please allow me to introduce myself before you pass judgment on all of us" came a tired voice from the back of the group. An older man was coming forward with a younger male not far behind him. Tracking his every step to be sure he was stable, the man placed one foot in front of the other.

'An older vampire?' Mina thought to herself, confused because most vampires in the race were young and didn't age. Watching him, she continued to think, 'He must have been turned when he was older. But why the limp? That would have gone away when he was turned. Unless his injury occurred afterwards. But even still.'

"My name is John, my son is Sam. I understand you got into a bit of a confrontation with these two a little earlier, is that correct?"

"Yes. And I'll happily do it again if deemed necessary."

"Well, I don't doubt that one bit, but I ask you to refrain from taking any action until you understand who we are."

"No offense sir, but I don't care to meet new people or be a part of something. The best thing to do is to leave the property and leave me alone."

"Allow me a few minutes. That's all I ask."

Mina refrained from rolling her eyes at the man due to respect for elders, even though she was most likely older than all of them combined. Relaxing a little, she dropped her arms and allowed the man to say his peace, not that she would exactly listen to it.

"We are a group of misfit vampires. We range from old to young even though we may not look it. My son Sam and his friend Dom are scouts for us. Looking to find any lone vampire in need of a home, food or company,", he continued. "We mean no harm and are not looking for violence."

Mina figured that when the two young males couldn't hold their own against her. There was no challenge at all towards her when she had given their warning.

"Once again, I appreciate you trying to look out for those less fortunate than you or trying to gather lonely vampires. But as I said, I'm fine being alone. And I have no issue with violence if the opportunity presents itself," Mina said to John and slightly addressed the others as well with the last part of her statement.

The older man of the group turned to his other members and looked at them. No words shared, just a look.

"We will leave you be, we want no trouble. If you change your mind, we are located a mile into the tree line headed northwest," John stated.

Mina didn't say anything and watched as they left her property. She closed the backdoor and walked back over to the old couch she was sitting on, sank down and picked her book back up.

After a few minutes, she set the book back down and began to think to herself. She thought of the older male and the young male and the other vampires who accompanied him. "They don't know how to defend themselves," Mina said into the quietness of the empty room. Of all the chances she had time to be a good person and help someone or multiple someones, why did she have a feeling to help them? A small group of outcasts who were probably 100% animal-only feeders.

Mina looked at the time and realised it was almost time for the sun to come out. She went on her phone and ordered some groceries through an app, paid with her fraudulent card, and scheduled the delivery time for 5pm.

After placing the order of just pure living essentials, she decided it was time to head back to bed. Walking up the old stairs to her room, she placed her phone back on the charger and climbed into bed.

Mina slept through the entire day with no interruptions. It was the sound of a vehicle entering her driveway that woke her up, yet she couldn't look out the window enough to see who it was. Judging by the clock on her phone, it was most likely the person delivering her groceries.

When her phone showed it was 6:45pm, she took a small glance out of her bedroom window and saw that the sun was gone enough to where she could be outside without any chance of an unwanted tan.

Opening the front door, she saw her groceries and other items she ordered. Bringing them inside, she placed the few bags onto the kitchen table and one by one placed things in their rightful place. Yes, even as a vampire, she still enjoys human food and can digest it.

Mina started a pot of coffee and placed some bread into the toaster. She drank her coffee black and her toast with just a little spread of butter. Nothing fancy, but just enough to hold her until later in the night when she got hungry again.

'7:20 pm' was displayed by an old clock on the wall, yet she checked her phone to confirm the clock was correct. After verifying the technology agreed with each other, she had one plan today: to go find that small group and see if she could at least teach them some survival skills.

She left the little farmhouse shortly after and began her walk through the lush green field, and headed north, just as John directed.

After walking for roughly ten minutes, she came across a campsite, 'This is definitely not safe,' she thought to herself. Unlike her and her special hand me down genes, typical vampires could not handle even the smallest amount of sunlight. They would in fact waste away like they were a piece of tissue paper in a wood stove.

Shortly after her arrival, she was met by a female who looked to be about 25. How long had she been that age? Who knows.

"Hey! I'm Jessica, can I help you?" the female asked.

"I was asked to give a chance to get to know you people, by John. Is he here?" replied Mina.

"Yes. We are actually all sitting down to eat together, if you'd like to join us."

"Sure, why not."

Reluctantly, Mina followed the young female over to a fire pit. She could smell eggs, bacon and a mix of fruit. Mina was shown to an open spot and took a seat as she waited patiently for John to make an appearance so she could get down to business.

"So you decided to join us after all", John said behind her. He was accompanied by that tall skinny male with the black hair. Sam? Was it? Right, John's son.

"I did, but this isn't a social visit. I wanted to offer some help with self defense. Just in case you come across some not so friendly people or vampires"

"Like yourself?" John chuckled as he spoke his words.

"Exactly."

"Well, allow us a few moments to eat our meal and then we can discuss this further."

John walked around to the opposite side of the pit where Mina had sat and was given a plate of food. The

same female who greeted her offered her food as well, but
Mina declined it.

"Can you tell us the story of the lost princess again?"
spoke a different female who was already done with her
plate and going to get seconds.

"I'd love to, as long as our visitor doesn't mind hearing
it while she waits."

Mina gave a nod of acceptance and allowed John to
tell the story.

"Once there was a family a long time ago, much before
our time, who resided in what we know today as Romania.
It is said that the king there had three daughters but no
sons. All his daughters had different personalities. One was
the leader, who knew her place and her duty to the race.
The next was kind and wanted to please her father by doing
as she was told. The youngest was a rebel who wanted
nothing to do with the rules of being a royal and wanted
nothing to do with finding a male, like her sisters."

Mina was slightly taken by the story, due to it hitting a
little too close to her than she would have liked. But she
showed no emotion, she gave no reason for them to think
she had heard this story before. They hadn't even known
her name yet. But she found it interesting that this vampire
knew this story and he definitely wasn't around when it
happened.

John continue., "Legend says that the younger daughter didn't want a male that her father had selected for her, so she chased after a forbidden love who worked in the stables. Someone had caught them sneaking around and told the king. The young daughter was to turn 16 the next day and the king threw her an extravagant ball to celebrate her coming of age".

As Mina continued to listen, she began to get restless, she didn't know how much more of this she could listen to.

"The king chose to give his daughter a birthday present, but the daughter didn't know that her present was her true love. It is said that her true love was-"

Mina shot up from her spot at the pit and began to walk away. She wouldn't listen to any more of this story since it was a play by play of her past. She already did not want to think about what happened all those years ago, let alone have some stranger talk about it like he was there.

"Have we offended you?" asked John.

"No, but I'm not here to listen to stories. I'm here to offer my help so you all don't get killed. If you want to continue your little camping trip, then so be it. I'll just be on my way."

Mina was surprised when Sam was the one who came up to her. Knowing not to grab at her, he said to her "Please, don't leave. Believe it or not, I'd really like to learn how to fight. Just in case". Mina looked back at him, reading his face, she could tell he was sincere in wanting to learn. She never noticed how blue his eyes were, like the tropical water in Bora Bora. Not that she ever got close enough to really see them.

She pulled herself back from her thoughts, "Fine. I'll stay. But you have to promise to do exactly as I say, or I'm gone."

"Promise," said Sam and he looked over to John who provided an agreeable nod to what Mina was proposing.

"Okay, has anyone here ever killed someone before?"

Looking around the group, not a single person raised their hand, and most looked concerned with her question. Continuing, Mina said, "Well, I'm going to prepare you for the day that you may have to. Whether it be for survival or for food, vampire or human."

As the group looked at each other for verification that they still wanted to learn what she had to offer, Mina looked over the male vampires.

"And you all will need to start feeding properly to help build muscle. Females can too but the males will bulk up quicker with the correct diet and training."

Sam and Dom were the first to step forward, then a few other males, and even some females came forward.

"Alright then, let's get to work."

<u>Eight</u>

Mina had been working with the small group for a few months now. Commuting back and forth between her farmhouse and their camp, Mina made it her job to have them training 24/7. She also convinced them to at least put up a type of 'roof' above the tents for added protection.

The 'trainees', as she called them, were coming along just fine. Some were progressing more than others, but small progress is still progress.

Mina walked along the 'training area' she had set up where those who chose to train could practice. She observed the males and females hitting their target, practicing hunting maneuvers, and gave advice for better tracking - whether that be an enemy or lunch.

No one ever questioned her after the outburst she had mid-story when she first joined them. Which was good, considering she had no good excuse besides impatience. In reality? She missed her family like crazy, and Di... she couldn't say his name. Not even in her head. He was her one love, no one could compare, and she never looked for anyone to replace him.

Shaking herself from her train of thought, she focused back on her trainees.

"Alright everyone!" Mina announced, "I've set up a test for you all to practice tracking. Find and return to me a small item that I've hidden in the field."

"What is it we are looking for?" came someone from the lineup.

"You will know when you find it. Use your skills and fight off whoever gets in your way. The winner isn't the one who finds it, but the one who places it in my hand."

As she watched them question each other like one may have info the other doesn't, she looked at her phone's clock so she could time them, and shouted "Ready, Set...... Go!"

Every single one of them burst forward from the line and immediately got to work trying to find where the mystery item was located.

In her mind, she was rooting for Sam to be the victor. She started to question herself as to why she had one specific male on her mind to begin with. She didn't care about him. She had no business getting close to anyone, especially a male. At one point, when she had first met Sam, he was a skinny male vampire who couldn't hold his own. Now? He was stronger - which showed under his now tight t-shirt - and faster. His tracking skills were showing improvement and his combat skills were almost worthy enough for an actual fight. At least he would have a chance now if he were to go against another vampire. Yet, she always made a mental note that the males should definitely be bigger than they were. They were still the size of a human, which when turned, would have changed since their overall build would have increased. Mina re-focused on the group instead of continuing her mental progress report on Sam.

A few minutes passed by and the field was filled with vampires, but each one was in a different location. Mina scanned the field and her eyes landed on Sam, 'Just a little to your right, you're so close, you almost have it' she thought to herself. Adding a comment in her head, 'Stop cheering him on'. It was like her brain was having a conversation with itself and she was just a passenger.

As soon as she said that, "Got it!" Sam shouted from the spot Mina was mentally pushing him towards.

Mina's hand met her face and she said under her breath, "Don't announce it…Keep it like a secret."

And with that, Sam was ambushed. Each vampire lunged towards him, kicking and scratching at him to get the prize. But, what do you know, Sam was able to manage his way out of the dog pile and began to run like his life depended on it. Mina chuckled a little and got serious again, watching the small group of vampires fall over each other while Sam was well ahead of them. Like sliding into home plate at a baseball game, Sam came in hot and handed Mina the lost item.

"There. Found it." Sam said out of breath, "What is my prize?"

"Prize? Oh. No prize, but you did lose points for announcing to the 'enemy' where you were and what you had found." Mina shook her head and walked away.

Sam took no time to catch back up to her, "Really? I get nothing? I found it first and out ran everyone. I feel like I deserve something."

Looking into those deep ocean eyes of his, she said, "Your life." Looking puzzled Sam raised a brow at her like she had spoken a language he had never heard before.

She explained, "If this was a life or death situation, and you announced yourself like that, there is a very high chance that a real enemy would have ripped you to shreds. So, your life is your prize."

"But it was basically hide and seek," he argued.

'Ok, this is getting childish' Mina thought to herself as she continued walking away, paying him no attention at all.

****

Sam was never the kind to let a female upset him. But when Mina just walked away from him like that, he wanted to grab her by the arm again and force her to explain why he would not be rewarded. Deep down though, he wanted her to be his reward. He wasn't sure why he wanted her, or what drew him to her, but he knew he wanted to be as close to her as possible.

"Mina!" He called after her, "Wait!" Catching up to her he was thankful that she stopped to wait for him.

"I'm sorry. I didn't mean to get upset over a little test. I've just never won anything in my whole existence and I was just happy to finally be a winner," he continued, "You're right. My life is the best prize to be won and I'm thankful for all that you have been teaching us this past month."

"You're welcome. Just try not to be so excited about it that you could get yourself killed in a life situation" Mina said as she placed her hands on hips.

'Kiss her. Just grab her by the face and kiss her,' he thought to himself. "Of course," he said, "Won't happen again."

"Good. Now go get cleaned up for dinner and I'll see you all tomorrow."

"Wait, wouldn't you want to join us?"

"No, I'm good, I'm going to go home and get cleaned up myself. A nice bath with a large glass of wine sounds good."

"That does sound good. Well, if you ever want any company, I'm here." After seeing the confused look on her face he quickly added "to hang out, not the bath and wine. Or maybe the wine, or the bath. I don't know what I'm saying anymore." Blushing, he turned away and started to walk back to camp.

"Well, I appreciate the offer," she called back to him while he continued to walk. Sam threw up his hand with his head hung low in embarrassment, "Anytime!" he replied.

After a few steps, he turned back around and watched Mina walk out of the woods and into the field until he could no longer see her. 'Run after her' his brain decided to comment, 'Don't let her be alone'.

Sam ignored the thought and resumed his walk back to camp for dinner.

****

Mina made it back to her house and immediately started thinking of how she could sense Sam watching her walk away and she wasn't bothered by it. The old Mina would have ruined a male for an unnecessary gaze at her. Yet, Sam was coming along quite nicely and Mina respected his devotion to learning how to defend. They all were. The whole lot of the trainees were gaining new muscle and becoming better with their movements. They were almost ready to be left alone and she could go back to living in solitude with no interruptions.

The idea though made her sad. Did she want to continue her tradition of living a solitary life? Constantly moving around so no one would recognise her or ask questions? Or did she want to start a new chapter with this band of vampires who were kind to her and welcomed her into their 'home' without question?

Mina pondered the thought of the possible new life she may live while she filled a wine glass with her favorite red and headed upstairs to her bathroom. The bathroom was that of a simplistic design but her favorite feature was the clawfoot tub that was positioned directly next to the window. She loved looking up at the stars - when they were out - and relaxing after a long day of teaching.

Mina started the water and turned both knobs, allowing water to run until the tub was just over half full. She removed her dirty clothing and threw them into a basket. When the water had risen to where she wanted it, she slid one foot in at a time and slowly lowered herself into the bath, and kept her hair up until she was ready to wash it. She only had an hour or so until the sun was going to make an appearance, so she took one more look into the night sky and decided to close the indoor shade.

Mina took her time with the bath, washed her hair and body, then decided it was time for bed. She didn't have much of an appetite since she began thinking about her possible new life, or what opportunities could come from all this. Did she want this for herself? Or for the possibility of getting closer to Sam? What was it about him that drew her to wanting to be near him? Heading to the bedroom, Mina dried off her hair and body with the same towel and hung it on the door to air dry. She slipped on some comfy shorts and threw on a v-neck shirt that was almost too low to wear in public.

Mina crawled into her bed that always announced when she moved around, and got cozy under the blankets. She didn't last long when her head hit the pillow, and she drifted into darkness.

****

"Mina!"

Hearing her name, Mina turned around and saw a figure coming towards her. She tried to get down into her fighting stance so she was ready for whatever was coming towards her. But when she went to get low, she felt a pull at her back and something prevented her from moving a certain way at her front. Mina looked down and saw she was wearing a red gown. The same gown she was wearing the day of her 16th birthday, the dress she wore to her coming of age ball.

72

"Mina!" the voice came again, but getting closer to her.

"Who are you?" Mina called back at the unknown person coming towards her.

As the figure got clearer and the calling of her name became more discernible, Mina realised it was a male calling out for her. Not just any male though.

"Dimitri?" she called out

"Mina!" his voice repeated

"What? Dimitri, what do you want? I'm here!"

It was as if he couldn't hear her, but he was still getting closer and closer.

Before she knew it, Dimitri was standing right in front of her. Looking down at her, gazing into her beautiful blue eyes. 'Blue as the skies' he used to tell her.

"My Mina, are you hurt? Are you okay?" he asked

"I am. Are you okay?" she replied

"I am fine now that I have found you, my princess" he said as he took her hand, "Don't forget about me, but don't hold yourself back, either. I want you to be happy. I want you to be free and not be scared of what's to come."

"What do you mean? I am here.....with you."

"You're not really here though are you? I'm only here in your memory. From a long time ago."

Mina felt her heart pull at her, realizing he was just a vision of her subconscious.

Dimitri spoke again, *"Don't be afraid of who you are and what you have been through. Own it, be proud of it."*

"But what if the council finds me? What should happen to me or anyone else who knows me."

"You are more powerful than you think, you stand in your own way."

Before Mina could get in another word, Dimirti stated *"My Mina I must go, I must leave you, but know I am always with you".*

Dimitri began to lower his head to her so their lips may come together.

Knock knock knock

"Whoever that is, I'll kill them," Mina said as she rose from her bed. She noticed that her eyes stung a bit and were wet. Reaching up to her face she realised that she had been crying. 'When was the last time she had cried about anything?'she thought to herself as she wiped the tears from her eyes. She had never had a dream like that in her 500 something years of existence.

Looking at the time she realised it was well past nightfall, so she sprung up and ran to the door down stairs. She was surprised, yet happy when she saw Sam standing at her backdoor.

"Are you okay?" he asked, "It's been an hour since your usual arrival time at our camp and I wanted to check on you."

"Yeah I'm fine, just overslept. You can come in while I get ready and I'll walk back with you," she said as she left the door open for him and made her way back upstairs. She grabbed her dark blue jeans and found a shirt she had already worn but it was only something she slept in once before. Rushing, she grabbed a pair of socks and took a quick look at herself in the mirror that hung in her bedroom. Looking at her eyes, she tried to use her cold fingers to get the puffiness to go down and blinked repeatedly to remove the redness around her rentinas. She didn't need Sam asking about her looks or assuming she was crying - even though it was the truth. When she returned, he was sitting at her table and didn't bother to move as she came into the room ready to leave.

"You ready?" she asked

There was no movement from him. Not a muscle twitch, nothing. Then he looked up at her and looked at her with concern and asked, "Why were you crying?"

<u>Nine</u>

Mina stood very still as Sam sat in front of her with seriousness and concern in his eyes.

"Don't try and deny it. I heard you before I knocked on the door", he said.

Had she been crying out loud while she was dreaming? Why had he been listening to her?

"I was just having a bad dream. That's all. Now let's go, we are wasting time sitting here talking about my emotions."

"What was the dream about?" he pushed, trying to get a real answer out of her, "I heard you saying 'Dimitri'. Who is that?"

"No one you need to concern yourself with. He is a memory, Someone from my past," she stated firmly. Not that it was any of his business, but perhaps that answer will make him back off so they can head off to the camp.

"Mina, I only ask because I care"

"Why? Why do you care how I'm feeling or what I'm thinking? What will you do with the answers I give you?" she said loudly with frustration.

"I wouldn't do anything with them except listen." He paused for a moment to allow her a chance to rebuttal. When he heard no words come from her, he added, "You are always so tough, so strong and confident in everything you do and say. Have you ever let someone in and let them care for you?"

"A long time ago."

"And what happened?"

"He died."

Sam looked at Mina like she was a hurt puppy who needed a good home to rescue it. Mina got stern with her voice, "Now, you can either follow me or stay here and try to figure me out. You won't, but I'm not going to stay here and wait while you make the effort. I'm leaving."

Mina walked out the backdoor and gave it a good slam. She was upset at Sam but more upset with herself for allowing her wall to come down a little. The dream with Di…. her thought stopped as she dropped to her knees in the field and began to cry. She cried with a power that she had not experienced in a very long time.

'Mina' came that all too familiar whisper that she hadn't heard since she moved in. Looking up, she tried to see if maybe there was a body with the voice, but once again, no one was around her. She stayed on her knees for sometime, just holding herself, trying to come back to reality and leave the dream behind. Yet all she could do was hold onto herself, as if she could float away at any given moment.

****

Sam sat in Mina's kitchen for some time before standing and walking to the door. Something felt off, although he didn't know what it was, but something definitely wasn't right. He reached into his pocket, pulled out his phone and shot a text over to Dom that read, 'Hey, tell everyone training today is canceled. Mina needs a break and she will be back tomorrow. I'll be back before sunrise." Sam hit send and slid the phone into his back pocket. He wanted to give Mina space but was unsure how far he was willing to push her. She was hiding something and for some reason he felt it his business to have her open up to him and come clean. Sam looked out of the back door window and saw Mina was down on her knees, hunched over, in the field. Before he jumped to conclusions about running out there to hold her or help her, he tried to listen to see if her breathing was level or if it was shallow. No, she wasn't hurt. He could smell the salt from her tears though and knew she was out in that field crying.

Sam gently opened the back door and walked towards his female. Er, Mina. He wanted to see if he could offer his support.

As he reached her, he heard her heartbeat pick up. She knew he was there, yet she didn't move a muscle. This was a good sign since before she would have fought him or taken off.

He reached down and decided to touch her shoulder. When there were no quick movements on her part, he lowered himself to one knee and just sat there with her. No comment. No advice. Just presence.

What felt like hours had passed by and neither of them had moved. Sam couldn't smell the salt from her tears anymore, so he assumed she had stopped crying. He wanted to say something to her but didn't know what to say. What do you say to a female like her, one who had been closed off for however long she made the choice to do so?

"His name was Dimitri," he heard her say delicately, "and he was the love of my life."

When Sam heard this his heart fell a little but didn't let that affect how he was going to be there for her in her time of need. He wanted to gather her in his arms and just hold her. To show her that he would be with her through every emotion and wasn't going anywhere.

"He was the one who last cared for you, wasn't he?" he asked kindly, "The one who died?"

She nodded her head but didn't say a word after that.

He continued with the probing questions. "Would you tell me what happened to him?"

Mina was silent for a moment and Sam gave her the time to answer when she was ready.

"My father." she was able to tell him, "My father had him killed for loving me. It's my fault he died."

"It couldn't be your fault. If you loved him and he loved you back, then it was mutual. Why would your father have him killed for that?" He wanted to know every single detail but also didn't want to push her too far.

With that, Mina stood up and he followed her lead. They walked back to the farmhouse and went to the living room where they sat together on the couch. He wanted to pull her close and put his arm around her, but chose the opposite end of the couch so she did not feel trapped.

"I think we need a day off from training", she mentioned.

"Already taken care of", he replied.

They sat quietly for a while, Sam assumed she was trying to find her words, so he began the conversation, "I was 28 when I was turned. I had no money, no home and I refused to move back in with my father. A man came to me one night while I was walking trying to find a place to sleep and he offered me some food and shelter. That was 40 years ago."

****

Mina lifted her head and met his eyes, '40 years?' She never would have thought that he had been around for that long. She figured he was a recently turned vampire when she had met him.

"So, do you like your new life?" she asked.

"I do, I was unsure at first but now I have a family, friends, a home, and now a really good teacher."

'Suck up' she thought to herself.

"When were you turned?" he asked.

She hesitated for a moment, not sure if she should answer him with a lie or the truth. Then she thought back to her dream, where her sweet Dimitri told her it was ok to move forward and not be ashamed of who she was, or scared to be honest. Perhaps he was right.

Mina took a deep breath, and looked to her left, through a large window that showed her the front driveway.

"I wasn't turned, I was born a vampire," she looked immediately to Sam as the words left her mouth. His look was that of curiosity, not fear.

"How is that possible?" he questioned.

"I have more to my story than just being a recluse vampire who doesn't care about the world or anyone in it," she added. "But I need to tell my story to everyone. It's time I was honest and I believe now is as good a time as any."

Sam got up off the couch, and extended his hand to her, "Then let us go together to the camp and you can share your story".

Mina took his hand, and followed him out the door. Yet she didn't let go of his hand. She held it till they were almost to the camp. When she did let go, he said " It's ok, I'm still here with you. Even though I'm also hearing your story for the first time, I won't judge".

"Thank you, I appreciate your patience and kindness," Mina replied with the faintest of smiles.

<u>Ten</u>

As Mina walked into the camp with Sam, Dom was the one to greet them at the entrance.

"I thought you weren't coming today. Did Sam finally make his move?"

Sam pierced him with a stare of 'shut up' which Dom quickly picked up on.

"Oh, um, nevermind, stupid thing to say. Well, you're in time to hear the rest of the story John was telling us a while back, want to join?"

"That's okay, maybe I should finish it for him. I know that story well," Mina replied.

Noticing the confused look on his face, she walked past him towards the fire pit. Dom turned to Sam, "What is she talking about?"

"I think we are about to find out who Mina really is," said Sam

"The doors opened as -" John stopped when he saw Mina. He hesitated before continuing in case she wasn't in the mood to hear any stories.

"Do you mind if I finish the story? I know it as well," Mina asked politely.

John nodded his head and got comfy in his seat. Mina sat down next to Sam and began to speak, picking up the story where John had left off.

"The princess was escorted by her father out of the double doors…" As Mina spoke, her mind drifted to that dreadful day and it all played before her like a movie.

****

The ball was boring for Mina. There were not many men she wanted to share a dance with. Except one, but unfortunately he was not allowed at these kinds of functions, even if he was to work as a server. Everyone, especially her sisters, was having a wonderful time as they danced with various suitors. Except Nataliah, she was dancing with the only male she was already promised to and wore a huge smile the entire night.

Her father had chosen many eligible males to take Mina's hand once she was of age, but Mina made sure that it was not an easy task for her hand to be won.

"May I have this dance?", a voice came from behind her. It was Henry, a male from England whom her father hand picked just for her. Mina looked at his hand as he held it out to her and she replied, "Yes, my lord." She was then led to the middle of the floor where they began to dance as the next song was played.

"Are you not enjoying yourself?" asked Henry.

"I am. It just isn't the place you would usually catch me on a night such as this. A night where the stars are out."

"Oh? And where might one find you on a night such as this?"

"Either a walk under the stars or in our library with a good book," she replied, hoping to bore him with what she considered fun.

"Ah, I, too, love a good book. Unfortunately I do not have the time to read these days," he replied.

Mina was slightly shocked to hear the male's response and it almost made her want to know more about him.

"What else do you enjoy?" he asked.

"Riding. I love to take my mount out and gallop through the field and the woods. I enjoy the solidarity of it and the freedom it brings."

"Well, if you'll allow me, I'd like to join you for one of your rides and share in such freedom."

Mina blushed slightly at the fact that someone had actually taken interest in some of the things she liked. Not even her own sisters or parents offered to accompany her on an outing.

"I do believe I'd enjoy your company," she replied.

The song had ended and the male bowed to her before parting ways.

Retreating from the open dance floor, Mina walked over to where her mother was sitting and joined her.

"Lovely night, is it not my dear?" she asked Mina.

Mina looked over to her mother and didn't say a word in reply. She didn't have to.

"My dear, I know you'd rather be down in the stables or in your chambers, but this is your night. Also try and remember that your father is doing what is necessary to secure you a fine male."

Her mother was right, Mina disliked it very much, but she was right. She had to find a male in order to secure her status in the world since there was a very high chance she wasn't going to take the throne. Princess or not, nothing was guaranteed.

As Mina gazed over the large number of people in attendance at her ball, her father announced over the sound of chatter, "Wilhelmina! My darling daughter! My youngest! Please join me here so I may present you with my gift!"

Mina smiled and moved through the crowd of people. As she passed, people bowed in respect for the new 'of age' princess and moved to the side so she could make her way through with ease.

"Yes, father?"

"Come now my dear one, let me take you to your surprise."

As the king nodded his head at the two male figures standing at the large double door, they opened it wide to reveal the outside. The night was beautiful and the stars were shining bright. Mina walked with her father and many of the additional guests out to the entrance of their home. At first, Mina was confused as she did not see anything that stood out like a surprise would.

"Father? I am lost, is my surprise to be out here? Or is it something I must go find?", Mina asked.

"Yes, my dear, do you not see? Look to the bridge that is connected to the town where our people reside. You will see your surprise there."

When Mina looked, she saw a large figure and a somewhat smaller figure standing beside it. Confused, she moved closer. After taking a couple steps, she gasped when she saw her Dimirtri standing next to that beast, Dragos.

"Father, I don't understand."

"Do you not? You have feelings for this boy, am I wrong?", he asked her.

"Father, I do, I love him. Is it my gift that you will let me leave here with him and make a life for ourselves now that I'm of age?"

"No girl, look closer."

Mina looked harder at the scene before her. Dimitri was not moving or calling out to her and he was motionless as he looked down at the ground. That's when she saw it, Dimitri had a rope around his neck that was tied tight and the slack went over the edge of the bridge.

Mina was flooded with emotions and didn't know what she should do or say to resolve things. Her mother and sisters had joined them outside and also saw the scene before them. Their queen mother had stepped forward and asked, "My king, why do you have your man out there with the stable boy? What wrong has he done to warrant such an execution?"

Distraught, Mina attempted to lung forward and save her beloved somehow from the impending death that awaits him. But, as she attempted her move, a very large set of arms grabbed her and she was unable to move from the guard's grasp.

"No! Father! Please! I beg of you, please do not punish him in such a way because I was careless with my heart. Let him leave from here, please don't end his life!" she begged.

"You shall not tell me what to do, you silly daughter of mine!"

As the king's words left his mouth, he looked up at his man and gave a nod. Dragos picked up Dimitri and threw him off the bridge and Mina heard the tightening of the rope as it took on the weight of her male. She could hear his breathing go from tense to silent in the matter of a moment.

He was gone.

Mina screamed and fought against the guards' hold as her mother held her sisters back so they couldn't interfere with Mina's punishment. She may have disagreed with her husband's choice, but she would not let it be known to the race.

"You have shamed me as a king and as a father by being disobedient and reckless with yourself," the king said, "and for that, you will be sent away until you have learned your place in this world. A place where silence is never ending."

A carriage pulled around with the same white horse that was prepared for her only yesterday by her dear Dimitri. Her father's guard threw her into the carriage and didn't allow her time to say goodbye to her mother or sisters. She was banished from her home for being in love.

****

As Mina finished her story, telling it as if she wasn't the one who experienced it, she looked around the fire and saw some saddened, some had tears in their eyes and some had questions.

John was the first to speak, "You told the story so well, so detailed. May I ask where you heard it from? Did you know someone who was there?"

"I knew the story because.....", she hesitated, "my real name isn't Mina."

The whole group looked at her now, puzzled and wondering what this had to do with the story she just told.

"My name is Wilhelmina Latislauve. The lost princess of the Transylvanian vampire race," she continued, "This story is mine."

****

Sam sat quietly while everyone talked amongst themselves and observed as Mina was waiting quietly for someone to ask a question. So Sam spoke first. " So, how long ago was this?"

"I was born April 27th..... Year 1494. And this story took place in 1510," Mina answered.

The whole group was shocked at this point as jaws dropped and a couple gasps were heard amongst the group.

"Well, now it makes sense why you're so good at fighting and hunting," Sam added in an attempt at some levity.

There were no laughs to be heard, just the casual cough or clearing of the throat.

"So, where did he send you?" a female asked.

"A convent in the next town over. The nuns would feed me but not blood, so I stayed weak and could not attack them. I was beaten if I spoke or did not complete my chores correctly."

"That sounds awful. All for love? That seems a bit extreme," the female added.

"It was the standard for someone of my status to follow the king's orders, father or not, and to marry someone of his choosing. Not mine," Mina replied.

Sam sat quietly while Mina answered questions and elaborated more on the details of what she went through. As if he could feel her become tense, Sam texted her so it wasn't obvious that he was becoming close to her, 'Hey, do you want to leave? Go for a walk?' He hit send and heard her phone vibrate as the text was received. He saw her reach into her pocket and nod while she kept looking at the others.

Sam stood up and began walking as if he was going to his tent, but changed direction to go deeper into the woods. He could hear Mina saying goodbye to the others, explaining that she needed to go home to relax a little. Once he knew she was walking toward the field, he changed direction so he could meet her closer to the farmhouse.

When he saw her walking, he stopped and just took in the sight of her. Mina had taken her hair out of its band and let it fall. He never knew her hair was so long or that it was the color of night. Her waves just subtly blowing in the breeze, like something out of a photo shoot. Then her eyes met his. Even though she was still a good distance away, he could tell that she wanted him to come home with her so she wasn't alone.

With that, they met at the back porch of the farmhouse.

Eleven

Sam and Mina stood there for what seemed like hours. Not talking. Just standing there in silence as Mina looked out into the field. It had been a long day for her, lots of emotions she hasn't endured in a long time. Speaking of things she promised herself she would never mention again, why was she so compelled by this group, and Sam for that matter, to give away her identity?

Mina almost forgot that Sam was still with her on the porch as she pondered her thoughts and feelings. It was kind of him to stay with her, but there definitely wasn't a need for her to be watched over. She had tried many many ways to take herself out of this world after Dimitri was killed, yet nothing worked, which is how she learned of her true immortality. Looking back now, she is slightly relieved that it didn't work, seeing as she would have never found Sam, or his 'family'.

She heard footsteps and decided to turn to see if he had decided to leave and give her space. But when she turned around, Sam was right in front of her. He was looking down at her, their bodies close, Sam was the first to speak.

"How are you?" he asked, with no selfishness in his eyes. He genuinely wanted to know how she was.

Mina hesitated before answering his question, "I'm good. Just a lot for one day is all."

"Would you like some alone time? I can leave and give you space."

"I, um….." She had to pause for a moment because she didn't really know what she wanted. "Will you come in for a little while?" she finally answered.

"Of course," Sam replied, as he began to walk toward the door, but waiting for Mina to be the first to enter her home.

"I don't have very much here, but feel free to sit on the couch or watch TV," she offered as she kicked her shoes off by the door.

"That's okay. I was thinking about dinner. I could cook for you if you'd like."

"Well, I don't have much here. I typically just hunt, but tonight I don't have the energy."

"Then you go up, draw yourself a hot bath and I'll figure it out."

"Really? You don't have to. I can still take care of myself, I'm just drained at the moment."

Sam slightly giggled to himself 'Of course she is still Miss Independent, even after today'.

Sam replied, "It's fine. Think of it as a thank you for teaching us how to fight and survive."

Mina shrugged her shoulders and walked away to go upstairs and start the bath as Sam suggested. She wasn't being rude, she just wasn't in the mood to go back and forth.

Mina went upstairs and grabbed the towels she had left hanging on her door, then headed to the bathroom. She started the hot water and began to undress. As she continued, she could see a body out the window. It was Sam. He wasn't facing her and watching her get naked, he was walking through the field. She honestly didn't care if he tried to turn around and see her through the window. His gaze on her was somewhat wanted, to have him look upon her body was something she would be willing to allow.

"Well, I guess he decided not to stay after all," Mina said out loud to herself. Stepping one foot and then another into the hot water, she could feel her body becoming more and more relaxed as the water consumed her.

****

Sam decided he needed to find something a little more substantial than just bread, coffee, and something that he assumed was fruit. Mina wasn't kidding when she said she didn't have much. Her pantry and fridge proved that she was, in fact, being honest.

Once he heard the bath water start, Sam walked out of the backdoor and began his mission through the field. He was going to put the skills Mina taught him to the test. His goal was an animal of some kind and to possibly swing by the camp for some vegetables. He wouldn't be seen since the garden was towards the back of the camp where no one stayed. Not that he was trying to be sneaky, he just didn't want to be bothered with questions of where he has been or about Mina.

Walking along, Sam found a trace of some rabbits nearby. He got low to be able to pick up their scent and looked in the direction he felt he needed to go and what do you know? There before him, a couple of rabbits were stopped, grazing upon the field, not realizing that a hunter was behind them. Sam made it a point to be as slow and quiet as ever.

When he felt he was a good distance away, he launched himself forward towards Thumper 1 and Thumper 2, and got both at the same time. They had no time to fight or flee, the kill was quick and effortless.

He did not feed off of them, so the blood could keep the meat fresh until he was ready to prep them properly.

Continuing on, he stealthily moved to the camp and found some carrots, potatoes, and green beans. As he collected what he required, Sam rose from his crouch and realized he was no longer alone.

"Hey, so you're stealing from your own people now?", came a female voice from behind him. Sam turned around to see a petite female about his age walking to the garden. How had he not heard her? Right. He was too focused on being quiet, he forgot his other senses.

"Not stealing, but yes, taking," he replied. He knew this female. Jessica was her name. She had joined his fathers camp not long after it was created. She always seemed to be close by when he took walks or sat to eat a meal, and she was friendly.

"Well, I won't tell if you don't," she said flirtatiously, moving closer and closer to him.

Sam didn't think anything of her advancement towards him until she was so close, Sam felt the need to take a step backward.

"Are you okay? Do you need something?" he asked her, confused as to why she was acting this way towards him.

"Oh, I'm fine, I just figured I'd come see what you were up to," she continued, "you know, if you ever need anything, I'm here for you."

Sam bent down and picked the remaining vegetables that he needed to feed himself and Mina.

"I'm fine, but thank you for the offer," Sam rose up and began to walk away.

"Wait!" she called after him, "Can I be honest with you?"

"Yeah, I suppose."

"I saw you walk back here and wanted to talk to you about something that's been on my mind since I first came here."

Sam stared at her with a confused look on his face.

Not making a comment to his facial expression, Jessica finished her statement, "Ever since I met you, I've always felt this undeniable attraction towards you. Something I could never fight off. I just feel like now is a good time to come clean."

Sam understood now why she moved so close to him and was always trying to strike up a conversation with him whenever Mina entered the camp. 'Since she'd met him?' All this close contact stuff with her didn't begin until Mina made her appearance.

"Jessica, I'm flattered. But I'm not really available at the moment. There's a lot going on and I'm just focusing on my training for now."

Sam turned to walk away so he could finally get back to the one female that did in fact have his full attention. Before he got too far away, he felt a grab at his arm.

"Please. I know you're going back to her. What does she have that I don't?"

She seemed mad now, and from a man's POV, her desperate voice was verifying that she definitely was not the female for him.

"I don't have to explain my choices to you. Now I've tried to be nice, but seriously, walk away."

Sam could smell her tears, and normally he would feel bad for treating a female like that. But in this case, he didn't care. All he wanted was to get back to that little white farmhouse and continue what he had originally set out to do.

He will deal with whatever drama Jessica decides to start, tomorrow.

****

The hot water was really just what the doctor had ordered. Sitting in her pool of relaxation, Mina closed her eyes and thought about her day. She didn't feel like shutting it away to some part of her brain for later. She wanted to direct it and understand it so she could face tomorrow. She knew the others would have more questions, she knew that those people would now view her differently, but she didn't care.

The one thing that did pop up into her mind was... "The council", she spoke out loud to herself. She had almost forgotten about the note she had received while she was living in Chicago. She started thinking of the possibilities they may have of finding her if more knew about her.

'Would they hurt those people?' she thought. 'Would they use Sam against me?' Mina's mind was running rapidly. All of a sudden, Mina heard a loud thud, like that of a door closing. 'Is that Sam?' she thought as she sat up in her bath.

He must have either heard her shift or he was a mind reader.

"It's just me!" Sam shouted from below.

Mina didn't bother to answer, she just laid back into her bath.

A few minutes later, she decided she had soaked long enough. Standing up she reached for her towel to dry off with. Not realizing she didn't pick up one of her feet quick enough, her body slammed down to the tiled floor of the bathroom. She may be able to heal rapidly, but she still felt pain. Mina let out a groan and began to pick herself up.

"Are you okay?"

She heard the voice coming from the other side of the door.

"Yeah, just got a little clumsy. I'm fine."

"Okay. Well, dinner is almost finished."

Dinner? What in the world did her figure out with the five ingredients her house held?

Mina pushed her body up off the floor and grabbed the towel she had originally planned on gracefully grabbing. Wrapped herself up and walked to her bedroom. 'Dammit', she cussed to herself, 'no clean clothes'.

Everything she could wear in front of company was dirty. It had been a while since she did laundry since she had been so busy with helping to train the others. Desperate, she found a long t-shirt, "Well, it's better than nothing," she stated as she grabbed the night dress and pulled it up over her head.

She gathered up all the dirty clothes and began to walk downstairs. She tried to be quick and get to the basement before Sam could see her. She glanced around the corner and saw him placing the final touches on dinner. 'Smells good whatever it is', she thought as she reached the basement door. Thankfully the door was located on the opposite wall from the stairs, so it wasn't much effort to get from A to B.

Quietly closing the door behind her and completing a balancing act of clothes with her other arm, she made easy work of loading the washer. She grabbed her little container of Gain, placed the detergent into the washer and closed the lid.

"These would have been so useful if we had them in the 14th century," she joked to herself. The gowns she used to wear would need modern-day dry cleaning more than a washer.

Mina traveled back up the basement steps and entered back into the hallway between the front door and back door. She rounded the corner and saw Sam sitting at the table, waiting for her.

"Well, don't dress up on my behalf," he joked.

Mina probably looked as close to homeless as she ever had. Hair up in a messy bun, no bra, no panties. Just the night dress that happened to be the one clean article of clothing left in her closet.

"Well, I mean, when someone takes the time to cook for you, you want to look your best."

They both laughed as the sarcasm was exchanged, and Mina sat down in the seat across from Sam.

"Are you hungry?" Sam asked.

"Starving. But, I'm curious as to what you were able to make."

"Nothing from within the house, that's for sure." He pointed to the meat that was placed on a tray, "That is rabbit. Caught, killed and cooked by yours truly," he then pointed to another dish that she recognized as vegetables, "And those are some fresh veggies from the camp's garden."

"You went back to the camp?"

"Yes. I knew our garden had plenty to spare, plus I wanted to make sure you had plenty to eat."

Mina had to fight her emotions so she did not start to tear up. No one had ever gone through this much trouble to make sure she was well taken care of.

"Is it too much? I can throw it away and take you out hunting instead. If you'd rather do things yourself."

Looking back at him, Mina quickly spoke up, "No. No, it's perfect. I was just surprised by all you had done while I was in the bath."

Well now, that just put a big smile on Sam's face. He picked up her plate and began placing the food on it neatly and placed the meal in front of her. He then did the same with his own.

The pair ate in silence, which Sam took as a good sign. When finished, Sam gathered up the dirty dishes and carried them to the sink. He was about to begin the washing process, since there was no dishwasher, until he was stopped by a hand on his arm.

"Don't worry about that right now. Why don't we go sit on the couch and relax for a little bit.

Without answering, he followed her to the couch and took a seat next to her. Not too close but not too far away either.

Crossing her legs once she sat down, she slightly turned towards him and asked, "So, when did you learn to cook?"

"I was attending cooking school before I turned. I was close to graduating and I had one year left when I lost my job and my funding for school," he answered.

"How did you lose your job? What even was your job?"

"I was a car salesman. Well, not a very good one obviously. But it paid the bills and helped with school." He looked down for the next part of his explanation, "I was let go on the premise that I was stealing from the dealership."

Looking at him with a puzzled expression upon her face, she asked, "you were stealing?"

He looked at her directly in her eyes, "No. They only thought I was. But they had a zero tolerance policy and took the word of my colleagues instead of looking for evidence."

Mina hated unjust punishments, and with good reason considering her past experiences.

He didn't let her reply, "I couldn't afford a lawyer and had no extra energy to fight it. I just assumed I'd find another job and be okay."

Mina had a sincere empathetic look on her as she closed the space between them and took his hand, "I'm so sorry that happened to you. Is that what made you want to turn?"

"No. Remember that man I told you about before? The One who found me on the street? Yeah, he took me in. I didn't know what he was at the time."

This made Mina raise a brow at him and prematurely began putting things together.

"He hired me to be his personal assistant. Told me he had a weird skin allergy to the sun and asked me to run errands for him. So I did. A few days after I began working for him, he knocked me out and I woke up with a whole lot of pain in my neck. It felt as though it was on fire, and it wasn't long before a form of throbbing began in my mouth. When I looked in a mirror and saw the bite, I thought I should go to the hospital, but instead I had these instincts that began to take over my mind. I could hear things as if they were right next to me, and see without imperfections. I had a craving that I couldn't shake, a craving for blood.

The man had a cat in his home and without giving it a thought, I grabbed it and fed from it. It was over so quickly, but it satisfied my craving enough that my mind wasn't buzzing anymore."

Mina asked a follow up question she had been wondering for a while, "And how did your father turn?"

"I visited him shortly after I turned and he told me that he was given some poor news from his doctor. He had a brain tumor and was given only a year to live."

"So you turned him to save him?" she probed.

"I didn't. But a few days later, after thinking about it, I went back to the man who turned me and asked him to help my father. After giving it some thought, he agreed to do it since I was so helpful to him while I was human."

Mina said nothing as she placed the pieces together, but a certain question was raised. Why were they all still so weak and slow (for vampires)? Even as a turned vampire, there are still benefits, and his father really shouldn't still have a limp when he walks. Mina sat quietly while contemplating her list of questions as she looked at Sam.

Sam had a look of shame from sharing his truth. As if he saved his father for his own selfish reasons, as if he didn't ask his father what he wanted.

"You did what you had to, to make sure your father continued to live," Mina told him, trying to ease him of his guilt.

"He was never upset with me. But I see him everyday and watch while he moves slowly. I know he doesn't feel the pain as much anymore, but it makes me question whether I made the right choice or not."

"I can tell you that you made the right choice. Because of your father being alive and his undeniable kindness, I was introduced to you. Well, all of you. The camp I mean." Mina spoke quickly so it didn't seem like she was only happy to have met him. Even though that was the real truth.

"No, your tight grip around my throat in that field introduced me to you."

They both shared a laugh at the fact that three months ago she was tempted to kill him for just being in her space. But now? She wanted him in her bubble.

Mina took a glance outside and realised it was almost dawn. "Well, the sun's coming up," she said.

"Guess I should get going before it's all the way up."

Mina looked at him with alarm. He wouldn't make it to the camp in time if he left at this point.

"I mean, I have a spare room if you'd rather just stay here. The sun is too close to being fully visible, I doubt your father would want you to take the chance."

"Are you speaking on behalf of my father? Or yourself?"

Looking up at him, she wondered for a bit. 'Would it be too much to ask him to stay? It is for his own safety, right?' She tossed the questions around in her head, but before she could return an answer....

"Sam!" shouted a voice from outside. 'A female? Outside? Now?' Mina thought as she and Sam looked at each other with confusion and alarm in their eyes.

Mina rose to her feet, but somehow Sam was the first to the door.

"Jessica?" Sam questioned as he and Mina came out to the porch, "What are you doing? The sun will be at full blast any second. Are you insane?"

"I won't live to watch you love another. I just won't." Jessica declared as she stubbornly stood there awaiting her fate.

"Don't do this. Just come inside and we'll talk" Sam begged as he could see a line of sun slowly closing in on her.

"NO! You choose now."

The sunlight was closing in on her, and Sam was being silent. Most likely thinking of something to say to get her to calm down. But time was running out and Mina was in no mood for drama.

'Stupid females,' she thought to herself.

Mina barged past Sam, grabbed the female by the arm and dragged her into the farmhouse.

"What are you doing?" Jessica yelled in protest.

"No one has time for your stupid games," Mina said, "Sam, do you want to be with her?"

"No, I don't," he stated, wondering if he could have been a little more gentle with the reply.

"Okay. There's your answer. And look, the sun is out and you're not in it. Guess you'll have no choice but to live now."

"I could just go outside. It's not like I can't operate a door knob," Jessica rebutted.

This time it was Sam who spoke up, "Jessica, please. I'm not the only male in the world. And threatening to kill yourself over it isn't the way to win me over."

"Then what can I do?"

Mina exhibited the biggest eye roll of her life as she watched the two go back and forth. Throughout the years, Mina was never one for drama and it drove her insane to watch a female risk her whole life over a male who didn't want them back.

"Well, I'll leave you two at it. I'm going to switch over my laundry and then go to bed. You kids have fun."

Mina walked off without giving anyone present a chance to speak to her or stop her.

While Mina finished things up with her laundry and started the dryer, she could hear the two upstairs yelling back and forth at each other. Until..

"Mina!" shouted Sam, "Mina! I need you!"

Mina shot upstairs to see Sam holding Jessica back from trying to bolt out the door. Annoyed, Mina said, "If she wants to kill herself like this, then let her. She seems to have her mind already made up", while she crossed her arms and leaned up against the door jam of the basement.

"Mina, please. I can't live with her death on my conscience," Sam begged.

Before Mina could make a move, Jessica put her newly learned attacks on Sam, loosening his grip enough for her to succeed in making a run for it. Mina saw the fear flash in Sam's eyes and decided she might as well just do it for him (though she didn't much care for the female at this point).

The sun was out and ready to claim a life, a vampire life that is.

Jessica reached the door, opened it wide and got to the top step of the porch stairs. Mina was right on her heels and was able to push the female back onto the porch, but her momentum meant she couldn't stop herself.

Mina tumbled onto the lawn and could feel the sun's warmth on her skin.

She could hear Sam desperately yelling after her, as if it was the last time he was going to see her. Little did he know that she wouldn't go poof into the air. But... she was seriously burned. Like that of an aggressive sunburn from laying out at the beach too long.

Mina had to make a move so she didn't roast any longer than she already had. Getting to her feet she pushed off the ground, causing her to go airborne and land with her back on the porch.

Things became blurry for her as that was the longest she had been in the sun in a long time. She could see Sam standing over her, yelling something, but she couldn't make out the words. Mina hoped he was yelling at that twit, who decided to make herself present without invitation.

That's when everything went black.

Twelve

The council had been relentlessly looking for Mina since she fled her last known whereabouts. The members of the council were at a standstill and not one of them had any idea of where to look for their missing princess.

"Have we checked with the mail carrier for a forwarding address?" the male called Gregor suggested.

"Yes. She has no mailbox or any record of her receiving mail," Vasile answered.

The three men continued throwing around ideas until one spoke with a thought that may actually be helpful.

"What about her cell phone?" Radu asked. Then, noticing looks of interest on the others' faces, which he took as support of his idea, continued "No one, human or vampire, will go around these days without a cell phone."

"Except us," Gregor stated.

"We are the exception. We have no need for a cellular contraption," answered Radu.

"What use is this cell phone to us?" came Vasile.

"Well, from what I understand, her phone is traceable. Which means we should be able to find her by tracking her cell phone," Gregor mentioned.

All three men nodded in agreement. Then one brought up a good point. "But, how do we go about locating her? What is the process to do this?" Radu asked.

"I'm not sure, but I shall ask the girl who tends to our place of stay," Gregor replied.

The Council had been residing in a small cottage, in the region of Transylvania, not too far from the castle the king once resided at.. No reason to leave the home they have always known. Until, of course, they discovered that the princess was indeed alive.

"Allow me a moment to fetch the young one," said Radu.

A few moments passed, and the council member returned accompanied by a young woman who was no more than 25.

"Well?" Gregor asked.

"Go on dear, explain," Radu stated.

The girl looked at all of them as if she had just entered some weird old man role playing game. Like 'Elders DND'.

The girl explained to them how it works and offered to show them on her phone how to do it. They explained to her that they have no device to do this process themselves.

Hesitantly, the girl decided to just find the phone for them. She didn't quite care as long as they kept paying her to clean their house from time to time.

"What is that?" Vasile asked.

"It looks like the phone is in the United States. Savannah, Georgia, to be specific. I believe I can get you an address if you want." The girl offered as she started tapping on multiple options with her finger. 'How odd,' Gregor thought to himself. None of the members would ever welcome new technology.

"Okay, it says she is at 164 Old Barn Road."

"It is done. We shall go and retrieve our princess and bring her home."

The girl looked around at the men and shared an expression of 'yeah, I'm going to go now'. She left them to whatever they were planning and closed the door quietly behind her.

The table in the center was already filled with old documents, signed laws, and, occasionally, a book or two. Pulling out a paper map of the United States, one of the men located the state of Georgia. With an address in their possession, they wrote a note.

"Another note?" Radu asked.

"What do you suggest we do? Send the girl?" Gregor rebutled

"No, we go ourselves. The last time we sent a note, the princess fled," Vasile commented

"There is truth in what you speak. Right, we shall go and retrieve her ourselves," Radu announced.

"With what, though? We have no modern transportation and we choose not to go onto those funny tubes that have wings." Gregor spoke.

The girl returned to see if the men needed anything before she left to go home.

"You! Take us to Georgia," Radu demanded.

The girl was stunned at the man's request. "I'm sorry, but I don't make enough money to take you to Georgia."

The men dismissed the girl so she could go back to her home and pondered what to do next.

"My fellow members, I do believe we must request the assistance of another. One of strength and honor," Vasile stated.

The other two looked at him, puzzled. "Of whom do you speak?" Gregor asked.

"The only one the king would trust to carry out the punishment if one were to break the law."

After a moment, Gregor spoke, "I believe you are correct. It is time to call upon the one who lay dormant beneath the castle."

The men wandered through the woods, following a path until it brought them to the clearing that presented them a view of the castle they once called home.

Someone had begun renovations in an attempt to restore it to its former glory, assuming they would use it to share the history of its former inhabitants.

Due to it being nightfall, there were no workers in sight. They made their way to the base of the rubble and found a passage that only few knew of, which led to the lowest level of the castle. There they found dead mice, some other unidentifiable carcass, and a body that resembled a large male. One stepped forward and made a small puncture in the pit of his hand. Blood presented itself, and the eyes of the male on the ground shot wide open. He had no energy to lunge at the old man, but could drink from a glass jar, until he felt more energetic. Only then did he ask "Why do you come here now? To bring me life after all these years?"

"We have a request for you. One which may bring you as much pleasure as it will us," stated Gregor.

"And what is this request?"

"Bring Wilhelmina home."

The male's face morphed into a large grin, revealing his elongated fangs.

"Tell me where she resides, and I shall complete this task."

Satisfied with the answers they received, Gregor handed a piece of paper containing the address to the male.

"Go now, and don't let anyone get in your way."

"Of course, my lord" the male bowed his head in respect and stood to his full height. He was well over seven feet and all muscle. He was a brick wall that no one wanted to get in the way of or challenge.

Gregor spoke up one last time before exiting the underbelly of the castle he said, "Good luck..... Dragos."

<u>Thirteen</u>

Sam was amazed, yet scared beyond belief, after he watched Mina launch herself at Jessica and fall into the sunlit grass. He immediately felt helpless since he couldn't be the one to go get her.

Somehow Mina had been able to get back to her feet and leap back onto the porch. He immediately went to her side and saw what the sun had done to her. 'How is she not dead?', he thought. Looking her over, her skin was bright red and peeling in some places. Her eyes were bloodshot and starting to close.

"Mina!" he shouted, "Stay with me, don't close your eyes!"

He watched as she attempted to keep her eyes open, but failed. He watched as her body went limp and her eyes closed. He could still hear her heart, so he knew she wasn't dead. Most likely unconscious due to the trauma her body endured from the sun.

Making sure to avoid her wounds, he gently slid his arms underneath her and raised her up. Like the protective male that he had become, he carried her to her room and lowered her onto her bed. Like something out of a magic book, he watched as her wounds began healing right in front of him. Her skin was already almost 100% back to its normal tone.

He decided to stay with her until she woke up. There was no way he would leave her side after what she had just done to save Jessica. Who was probably down there on the porch still, but he didn't care anymore. He shouldn't have let her control his good side like that. After all was said and done, he wouldn't be bothered if she walked out into the day. He didn't care about anyone else, except his Mina.

"My Mina," he said with a purr in his voice, which declared his love for her.

He no longer corrected his thought pattern about his feelings. Not after he thought he was going to lose her. Sam took her hand in his and laid his head on the bed while he waited for her to wake up.

After many hours had passed, he felt Mina begin to stir on the bed. Picking his head up to look at her, he saw her eyes slowly open.   .

****

Mina felt herself begin to regain consciousness and tried to move her limbs to wake herself up more. She felt a hand on hers, 'Sam?', she thought to herself, 'Has he been here the whole time?'

Mina attempted to open her eyes so she could see, but her eyes had been badly burnt by the sun.

Blood.

She needed blood to fully recover from the damage she essentially inflicted on herself. Well, it was for Sam wasn't it? She lifted her free hand to her eyes and tried to rub away whatever was causing the blurred vision, but they were still sensitive to the touch.

She realised there was a light on in the bedroom. 'It must be nighttime,' she noted in her head. She couldn't move too much, and she couldn't see. Perhaps she should try speaking. Clearing her throat she said, "Turn off. The light."

Mina's voice wasn't raspy, it was her lips that didn't want to work properly. Still slightly burned, her lips felt like they were glued together.

Blood.

She needed Sam to go out into the night and bring back, not animal blood, but human. It was the only thing that would help her heal quicker. Not that she was on any kind of timeline, but because she didn't want to lay around like a paperweight for a few days. If something like this was to happen to her and she was alone, she would have forced herself past the pain and hunted. She didn't care who or how old, she would obtain what she craved most.

"Blood." Mina was able to say, "Human."

She could sense Sam's hesitation to act on her request, but then it faded quickly and she felt him release her hand and walk out of the room.

Mina decided to close her eyes and drift off while she waited for her male, er, Sam to return.

After what seemed like a short nap, Mina awoke from the slamming of the front door. She assumed it was Sam, or at least she hoped it was him. She would fight if she had to, but really didn't want to move from her current position of rest.

That's when she smelled it. The iron that resided in what he carried into the house was so strong. The scent alone brought some life back into her.

After a short moment, Mina felt Sam brush something wet onto her lips. Using her tongue she slid it back and forth across her lips and the taste that registered in her brain was like a bolt of lightning going through her.

'More.'

The word ran through her mind like a CD skipping over and over again.

Mina sat up and grabbed what she assumed was a jar, and threw its contents straight into her mouth. She ingested the contents of the jar with speed as if it had been years since she last fed.

As she gave the glass back to Sam, she noticed her vision was perfect again, her skin fully healed, and she felt brand new.

"Thank you," she said to him. "That was exactly what I needed. I appreciate you going to get this for me."

She swung her legs over the side of the bed and waited for Sam to respond. But no words left his mouth and he had a look of shame upon him.

"Are you okay?" she asked, with noticeable concern in her voice.

"I'm…. fine." Sam said, with a hint of guilt in his voice.

"That was your first time collecting human blood, wasn't it?"

When she saw Sam nod in agreement with her assumption, she took his hand and said, "I know it has a different effect on us, to take from a human rather than an animal. But it's also what we need as vampires. We are the predator and humans are our natural prey."

"I went after the first person I saw. I had no conscience while doing it. I just knew I had to get you better again."

Sam looked down at his hands, which were placed in his lap like he was a child who had done something he shouldn't have.

"She was an older woman", he continued, "maybe 80 or 90, just up the road. I figured she was on the brink of her end anyway, but I made sure she didn't see it coming and it was quick."

Mina sat up a bit from her former slouched position and began to realize who he collected from. But she couldn't tell Sam that. She could already see what an impact taking his first life was having on him. He needed time to recover before the truth could be presented.

'Does this mean I stop paying rent?', she asked herself jokingly.

Not giving the housing question anymore thought, she turned her attention back to Sam.

"It's okay to be sad your first time. But, I can promise you that the health benefits of drinking from a human instead of an animal is very worth it."

"Nothing is worth taking a human life," he said bluntly. Mina had to take a second before being too harsh on him and remind herself that she had been doing this since birth. Sam wasn't presented with a choice or anything. Not that she had one either, but it was her normal.

"I understand how you feel. And, I'm fully grateful for you doing this so I could recover quicker. But, please do one thing for me. There is a small amount of blood left in that jar. Just try it."

He looked at her with an 'are you kidding?' expression on his face.

"It's not like you're killing again. You're actually just not wasting the last amount. So, in a sense, you didn't kill for nothing. Please, just trust me." Mina spoke before Sam had the opportunity to argue.

"Fuck it," Sam said as he placed the jar to his lips and threw his head back as if he was taking a shot.

What happened next was a total surprise for both Mina and himself. Immediately after swallowing the small, Sam lowered the jar from his lips, and Mina thought to herself, 'Did someone increase the temperature in the room?' as she began to feel like the room was becoming a sauna.

Looking at Sam, she noticed he looked like a whole other person. His kind eyes were narrowed and she could hear his heart begin to race.

"Sam?" she asked out loud, concerned he was about to have the vampire equivalent of a heart attack.

No answer came from him. He just stared at the bed with a blank expression on his face. His breathing was increasing and she could tell he was thinking about something. She could sense a sort of emotion or hunger radiating off him, one she hadn't felt since she met him.

'What was in the old lady's blood?' she wondered. Mina slowly got up off the bed, and moved around Sam.

He remained seated at her bedside, as if he didn't realize her absence, and Mina made her way to the door.

Once she reached the hallway, she turned around to see if he had moved and discovered he was right behind her.

"What the fu-", Mina was cut off from finishing her statement by a large hand coming to her throat and slamming her against the hallway wall.

Sam was practically towering over her, as if he had grown a whole foot in seconds. His sheer presence radiated that of a male claiming what was his.

'That's what he is going to do, isn't he?', she thought for a split second.

The thought tailed off as she became distracted by the muscles protruding from his shirt. Mina took her hand and trailed it up his extraordinarily muscled forearm and to his hand.

"What's your next move, big guy?" she asked, her voice flirty and suggestive.

"You're. Mine." Sam responded, his voice deeper and more demanding. Gone was the innocent, caring, guilted man from only moments ago.

'I'm yours,' Mina thought to herself. She tried getting the upper hand on him and wanted to take control of the situation. But her strength was no match for him as he pinned her against the wall again to show control. Of course, he was only able to because she allowed it, but she didn't mind seeing this possessive side of him.

"Don't fight me," he growled, "I'll let you take the lead, but not until I'm finished with you."

Mina usually never let others control her, but this male before her was doing everything except turning her off. She could feel herself grabbing at his clothes as she wanted nothing between them. But that wasn't Sam's plan. No, she could see it in his eyes that he wanted to take things nice and slow.

Sam dropped the hand he had braced above her and moved it to her lower back, then down to her ass, and he made his way under her large t-shirt. Mina gave herself a mental high five by going with no bra and panites earlier. Not that any were clean anyway....

"Don't move," he commanded her. He grabbed a handful of her ass and then traced his hand around her hip to the front of her lower abdomen.

"This is mine now," he said, as he began to slowly slide his hand between her legs and began to part what was blocking his path.

Mina lost it. Feeling herself panic, she reached into her strength and quickly maneuvered herself away from Sam and got him to the floor. She had him face down, arms behind his back, and her fangs fully extended. She let out a slight hiss and didn't let him break free from her hold while she straddled him.

Sam's masculine trip calmed right down as he said, "Okay, okay,,I'm sorry. Too fast, too soon."

Mina jumped off him, as if she didn't realize what she was doing until she had already done it.

Sam slowly raised himself off the floor, but to his surprise, it wasn't as difficult as he was expecting.

"Wow, you were right. I guess there are some benefits to human vs animal." Sam went silent after looking over at Mina, who had thrown herself into the far corner of her room.

"What's wrong? I'm sorry if that was too much. I felt no control in my actions for some reason."

Mina looked up but not at Sam. Lowering her eyes once more, she looked disappointed.

"Please, tell me how I can make this better for you," he begged her as he went to her and got down to her level.

"No, no, it's not you. Well, it is you. It wasn't what you were doing or what you were saying. I liked all of it. It's just...", she trailed off, she didn't know how to explain her headspace to him.

"I'll understand, I just want to know what happened."

In her silence, Sam began putting pieces together he felt would fit to show the reason for her resilience.

"It was him, wasn't it?" he inquired. "Your first love? It was his memory that made you want to stop."

She looked up at him, wanting to disagree with him. But she couldn't, because he was right. The last time Mina was touched like that by someone that she actually cared for, or who cared for her, was Dimitri.

"I'm not upset, I can't be. He was your first love. The first love always leaves an imprint on us that never goes away."

Upon hearing this, Mina's eyes began to fill up. But she caught herself, no more crying. She shook her head clear and replied, "Thank you, I appreciate that."

"Can I ask a question, though?" Sam requested.

"Of course."

"One day, will you allow me to finish what I had started?"

"Absolutely. Your inner beast side is quite a turn on."

"Oh," he purred, "I could tell." He ended his statement with a wink which made her smile shyly.

"What was that, though?" he asked, "Was that solely because of the human blood? Or, was that like a mental overload?"

"From what I've seen, male vampires who have been turned need human blood to fully complete their transition."

"Well, does that mean I'm a full vampire now? What was the last 40 years then? Practice?"

"Wait, you've never fed off a human before?"

"Not till tonight, no. When I turned, it was a cat that I fed from."

Minas' mouth dropped open. "Damn, so yeah, I guess this version of you is your vampiric side."

Sam rose up from his crouched stance and walked to the mirror. His features seemed the same but he had more muscle and more height to him. He was a full blooded predator now. Just the sight of him would cause any living creature to instinctively take notice, whether from lust or fear.

Mina continued to sit in the corner of her room and watch as Sam admired his 'new' self. She admired the view as well.

Then she asked, "Wait. Has anyone at your camp ever fed off a human before?"

He turned back to her and said, "No."

<u>Fourteen</u>

Mina didn't know too much of the whys and hows the transitioned vampires had to go through. But it was slowly becoming clear as to why the group at the campsite was so scrawny for vampires. Why it seemed if something came after them, they wouldn't be able to hold their own.

Sure, her training helped give them skills, but she had also expected them to be stronger or faster than they were.

A few hours had passed since their little semi-happy incident upstairs. Mina and Sam had made their way downstairs. It was an hour or two from daylight making an appearance and they had a lot to talk about. Talk about what they were, what needed to be done, and figuring a way to get the group on board with feeding on humans. Sam was sitting next to her, helping her fold clothes, both just sitting in the silence.

"So, I was thinking…. Would you like me to teach you to hunt like a pro?" Mina suggested nonchalantly.

"You mean, hunt people, right?" Sam clarified.

"Yes. It's in our natural instincts as vampires to hunt those who have a time limit here on earth."

Sam shrugged, "I guess. I just don't know how the others will take it."

"I feel as long as they see what it did for you, they will be fine with the idea."

"You do realise it's like asking vegans to eat a steak, right?"

Mina laughed, "But it does happen!"

They both shared a small chuckle while continuing on with the clothes.

Mina wasn't bothered by him helping her, she actually found it attractive. Even when he would handle her panties.

They finished the clothes and Mina took the load upstairs to her room, where she put them away quickly so she could return to Sam. As Mina came back downstairs, she saw Sam at the backdoor. He had his boots on and seemed like he was making a break for it.

"Where are you going?" Mina asked.

"I've got to go check on everyone. I haven't heard from Dom in a while and I just want to make sure nothing has happened."

"Oh, okay. Well, I can come with you if you'd like."

"That's okay, I'll be back before the sun comes up. I've got an hour 'til sunrise. You can time me," he said with a wink as he walked out the door and began jogging towards the camp.

"Well, at least his energy is up," Mina commented to herself.

****

Sam made his way back to camp and was happy to see that everyone was doing their normal routines. Checking their covering to make sure there weren't any holes for sunlight to pass through, cleaning up after dinner and doing a last head count before going to bed. The last was a security measure to make sure no one wandered off and got caught in the daylight with no shelter. His father had always cared about others' safety and well being, even before he turned.

When Sam entered the camp, it was like he came in doing a jig with some kind of weird hat on his head. Everyone, and I mean everyone, looked up at him like he was a being from another planet.

Dom was the first to approach him, "First of all, where the hell have you been? And second, where did you get the body upgrade?"

"I'll explain later, but I can't stay. I just wanted to come check on things and my father. Then I'm going back to Mina's."

"So…. You finally made your move?"

"Well, not exactly. It's a long story."

"But you two are together now? Or are you getting private lessons in other 'defensive maneuvers'" Dom ending in air quotes definitely made Sam smile just a little. Sam had an image from only hours ago flash across his brain and made him almost ready to try again.

"No, nothing like that. Just trying to help her while she comes clean with who she is."

"Well, aren't you just a sweetheart," Dom teased.

Sam decided to walk off with a laugh and resume his mission to find his father and then head back to the farmhouse.

"Well hot damn! Get a load of this guy!" One female called out, which attracted pretty much everyone in the camp who contained ovaries. The males rolled their eyes and continued on with their duties.

The questions came flying around him from all sorts of directions. There were only five females, but right now it would seem like twenty. A lot of their questions involved his looks and if he was still single, and one asked if he would put a baby in her. Sam skillfully removed himself from the swarm and made his way to his fathers tent. The females did not follow, most likely due to them conversing with each other about his new looks.

"Dad?" Sam called as he drew back the tent flap.

No sign of him. Weird. Sam pondered where he could be at with it being this close to sunrise.

"Hey!" he called to anyone who could answer him, "Has anyone seen my father?"

Everyone looked at each other and began to call out. No answer. No sign that his father was even at the camp.

'John' was being called from different people throughout the forest. They had minimal time before they had to seek shelter.

"Dad!" Sam called out desperately. Something wasn't right. He could feel it, unless that was a new sense he acquired from ingesting human blood.

He began tracking, starting from his fathers tent and seeing if he could pick up a scent for some kind of direction. Nothing.

Sam was getting annoyed,"No one saw him leave at all?", Sam asked out once more and everyone shook their heads. Except, Dom. Sam rushed over to his friend and immediately started grilling him on what he may know or what he could be hiding.

"Dom, where is he?"

"I don't know Sam, I promise."

"Liar!"

Sam grabbed his friend by the shirt and picked him up off the ground, "Tell me!"

Around him, people gasped at what they were witnessing. The once smallish male who had minimal muscle and a normal build, was now able to lift someone with one hand and no effort.

Sam ignored them, "Tell me or you'll become a personal s'more!"

Dom had never been threatened by his own friend before. He wasn't mad though, because he knew Sam was just scared that he may never see his father again.

"Listen," Dom said with fear, "he told me not to tell anyone. He said he was going for a walk to clear his head and he will be back by sunrise. That's all! Now put me down you lumberjack!"

Sam set his friend down and tried to think of where his father would walk to.

The sun was coming out. His time was up.

****

Mina was washing up the dishes from the dinner the night before when some feeling shot through her. It was like she was about to lose someone, but who did she have to lose? Sam?

Mina was in the process of pulling her phone out of the nightshirt's pocket, but before she could dial, a call came in. The screen read 'unknown caller', which she typically would ignore, but something in her gut said to answer.

"Hello?" she said cautiously.

"Mina, it's John....Sams father."

Fifteen

Transylvania, 1510

The smell of smoke entered Dragos' nose while inhaling the night air as he approached the king's castle in Transylvania. After three long days of travel to complete a task for the king, he was happy to be back home. Since he was a young male vampire, Dragos was one you never wanted to cross. He was born a vampire and wasn't much younger than the king himself. Dragos was raised to fight, kill, and protect. Always loyal to his king and he never backed down from any task.

Passing through town, it didn't take him long to arrive at what was supposed to be the castle gates.

'Where is everyone?', he questioned in his mind. He made no noise in case the enemy was still present and kept to the shadows.

He could tell that it had been at least 24 hours since the attack, due to the state that everything was in. The smoke was still prominent from the wood accents of the castle that had burned and the debris of the castle's stone walls.

He searched everywhere for his king and queen, even the princesses, but they were nowhere to be found. The thought of suicide crossed his mind as he searched for the royal family. With his main job being to protect them, he had to keep looking. If they were no longer around, who would he protect now? No. He would not think of that, just in case someone had by chance survived.

Deciding he didn't have much to do, no one to serve, until he could locate the royal family, he thought of the princess, Wilhelmina. She would not have been present at the castle because her father had sent her off to the convent nearly a year ago.

'Could she have done this?' he thought. Dragos was never fond of the youngest princess. He despised the way she disobeyed the king and made a fool of herself with that stableboy.

He began his journey up the mountain to where the convent resided. It was a small place, with no noise, and bodies moving slowly around the grounds.

Not knowing the correct protocol for entering the convent as a male, he decided to just knock on the wooden gate and ask for her.

A small human woman came to the gate but would not allow him access.

"The young princess is not here, she left the night before," the woman spoke, no shake in her voice. She was not nervous of him, not a shred of fear made her heart race or her body tense.

"Where can I find her?" he pushed.

"I'm not sure, she fled whilst the rest of us were sleeping. We went to her chambers to bring her food and she was nowhere to be found."

Dragos took one more scan of the convent grounds through the spaces in the entrance gate, and left.

'Perhaps she did go back to her family and escaped or perished alongside them,' he thought, trying to figure out his next move.

"Stupid girl," he commented.

But, then he remembered that at the current moment, if she were alive, she was the one who would take the throne and be the leader.

Dragos made his walk back to the place where the castle once stood strong and did a quick perimeter check. No bodies, animal or vampire, were found. Dragos began removing bits of debris from a specific spot near where the castle wall once stood. He bent down at the waist and lifted two wooden doors that somehow survived the fire, which revealed stone steps leading down into a dark tunnel.

This was one entrance to where the old dungeon was located. He had been there many times before, but with the little markers destroyed it was difficult to find. Once he entered he tried to find any sign that possibly the royal family had made their way down here where they could have been spared. Yet, there was still no sign of them. Becoming extremely discouraged, Dragos decided to allow himself to go into a deep 'coma-like' sleep until someone could wake him to resume his duties. If anyone thought to search for him down there, that is.

He decided to find a place on the floor of the dungeon and close his eyes. He struggled at first to drift off, but once successful, the centuries passed quickly.

****

Transylvania - present day

After the three men left, Dragos was unsure how to get to the princess and how he would approach her after all these years. He needed strength, which meant he needed to hunt.

Making his way out of the basement, he discovered the sun had fully descended and the light from the moon was at large. Taking a look around, he saw strange yellow monsters that did not breathe or move to look at him. He found a small object on the ground near the top of the dungeon's steps with a note attached to it.

"Use this to call us when you find the princess. All you will have to do is use your finger to push down on the green square twice to call us."

- *The Council*

Dragos folded the note up and slid it into the back pocket of his pants. To his right there was a small rectangular building with a large type of candle lit. He could hear voices speaking and decided to advance and see who it was. Once he reached where the voices were, he wasted no time investigating who was inside.

Three men were surrounding a desk that had multiple pieces of paper on it and they seemed to be disagreeing about something. One looked up and noticed Dragos had entered and began asking questions, "Who are you?" and, "What are you doing here?"

Dragos wasted no time in answering the questions by immediately advancing on the men and killing them, one right after the other. Of course, once he got his fill he was pretty much back to his original self. Feeling his strength and stamina return to him, he decided to glance over what the men were discussing.

'Nighthawk Construction' was a title on one of the papers. He didn't quite understand what he was looking at or reading at first, but he slowly pieced together what was in front of him.

"They are going to rebuild?" Dragos questioned out loud to himself. He figured out he was looking at plans. Plans to rebuild the king's home, but there were rooms drawn in the wrong location. Although tempted, Dragos decided it was not worth the time to fix, especially since he could be using that time to find Wilhelmina.

Dragos looked back over at the men and noticed that they were dressed very differently than he was. Assuming things have changed drastically since the 16th century, he looked around to see if there were any clothes that could fit him. He found nothing, so he decided to just slightly modify his current wardrobe. He was currently wearing black pants that were tucked into boots, and a loose black shirt that covered his arms all the way to his wrists. He also had a long black cape to keep warm.

Ditching the cape, he decided it was much too warm out for a need of a covering. Using a knife he found on one of the men he had fed off of, he cut the sleeves off this black shirt to match another man's shirt. The short sleeves showed his arms and Drogos was slightly taken by that. He had always covered his arms. That was always deemed proper for those days. He assumed now, less is more comfortable. His pants were too tight to wear over his boots, as suggested by the man wearing the short sleeved shirt. He wore a light blue, stiff material that covered the tops of his boots. Dragos pulled his pants from his boots and gave the inside seem a slight cut to widen the bottom cuff, which allowed his pants to then cover his boots. Making these slight modifications, besides color, made him look more modern than his past clothing.

Feeling like he was finally ready to begin his mission, he then questioned himself, "What is 'United States of America'?"

Dragos pulled out the small rectangular object from his pocket and did as the note instructed. After doing so a voice came from it, "Hello?" the voice said, "Dragos? You need to speak as well for us to talk."

"Yes, I'm Dragos," he answered awkwardly.

"What do you need?" Gregor asked.

Dragos asked his many questions of the world and how he should travel to this place he had never heard before.

Once he had his answers and was given some additional information, he was ready to begin.

Dragos began walking to a small building that had planes and found a small man standing with a sign for Dragos. Apparently some of the king's gold had been found by the old men and was used to buy a jet.

"Are you Dragos?" the small human man said.

"Yes."

"Wonderful, Follow me."

The man led him to a small plane which would take him to his destination. Little did Dragos know that there was much more to his trip than a simple plane ride.

<u>Sixteen</u>

"John?" Mina said into the phone. She was confused because why would John need to speak with her?

"What can I help you with?" Mina asked.

"There is something I need to talk to you about and I wanted to do so when you were alone," John replied.

"Oh, well you're in luck. Sam just left to go check on everyone at the camp and see you."

"Yes, I figured he'd do that, so I left and have been waiting here for him to leave. May I come in?"

"Oh, you're here already? Yeah, come to the back."

Mina walked to the backdoor and let John inside. Realizing that she was still in a nightshirt, she bolted upstairs to throw on some shorts and a t-shirt.

"Sorry about that, I wanted to put something more appropriate on," Mina said as she came back down from her room.

"Not a problem. Is there somewhere we could sit and talk?" John asked.

"Yes, right over here at the kitchen table."

Mina showed John over to the table and offered him a cup of coffee, but he refused. She sat down across from him and allowed him to start speaking so he could say what was on his mind.

"Sam doesn't know this, but I have known about the vampire race since I was a young boy. Stories and legends had been passed down from generation to generation. As far back as I could find, our family tree began in Transylvania." He paused before continuing, "As I began digging for more information about vampires, Sam came home one day and he seemed different. I could tell that he had changed into one of them. He was more pale than usual but still his energetic self and didn't seem sickly. I'm not sure if he told you, but that same day I was diagnosed with stage 4 lung cancer and I had a clot in my leg causing me to develop a limp due to constant cramps. Once Sam heard this, he left and returned a few days later with this plan to just make everything better."

Mina listened as John continued on with his story. She saw him begin to seem unsettled by what he was about to admit.

"Please, continue," she encouraged.

"Well in my research, I discovered that part of being a vampire was to feed off humans. So when I turned I told Sam of our family history and informed him that information had been passed down. Soon the topic of what vampires live on came up."

"Did the man who turned you two not tell you the ins and outs of being a vampire?"

"No. He simply provided that which was needed to turn and left us to our own demise."

Mina began to think more as to where this whole conversation was going and why he felt the need to tell her all this.

John continued, "Sam figured we had to feed off blood due to all the vampire movies he had seen, but he didn't know it had to be a specific kind of blood. He asked what kind and I told him animal blood would do so that we didn't have to kill anyone."

"But….. you knew the truth. You knew that human blood was needed," Mina responded, her voice taking on an accusatory tone.

"Yes. I knew. I figured life would be easier if he didn't think we were monsters and that we could still live a very simple life. I also told him that the best thing for us was to move out of our home and to the woods where no one would search for us."

Mina stood up from her seat and walked over to the sink where there were still some dishes to be done. Looking out the window at the sky becoming brighter and brighter, she spoke, "John, I have one question for you and I really hope I'm wrong about what the answer may be." Not waiting for a reply, she continued, "Did you know that in order to complete the transformation from human to vampire, one has to drink the blood of a human?"

There was a brief pause after she asked her questions and then came a firm, "Yes." from John.

Mina dropped her head and began getting upset. "And did you purposefully not tell Sam and the others of this?"

"Yes."

She turned to him now, facing him, "Why?"

He looked away from her, "When I turned them -"

"WHAT?" Mina said as she cut John off, "Wait, you turned all those people at the camp?"

"Yes. I turned them so Sam would have a community if anything were to ever happen to me. People who could follow him and he would have friends."

"And you withheld the one thing a vampire needs to be strong. Why?"

"Because I didn't want any violence. I figured that keeping them from fully turning would keep them still partially human. For Sam's sake."

"John, this makes no sense. So you created your own community of vampires, starve them of the one thing a vampire needs to be able to defend themselves and survive, then say it's so Sam won't be alone?"

She did not mean that to be rhetorical, and she waited for him to confirm the truth.

"Yes, that's correct," John confirmed.

"That has to be the most ridiculous, 'cult' like thing I have ever heard. I'm not sure if you saw Sam leave, but he's a fully transitioned vampire now. He told me he never knew about needing human blood to fully transition. That's probably why he left here to go talk to you before sunrise."

Mina was beyond heated and she was wanting so badly to kick him out of her house and go tell those people the truth. But the sun was slowly rising and he would not make it back in time.

Almost immediately after she considered kicking John out, Mina's phone began to ring.

"Hey," she said as she saw it was Sam who was calling her, "Yeah, he's fine. He is sitting here in my kitchen telling me some stories of the past. Yeah, he wants to talk to you. I know, the sun is out. No, stay there. I'll see you tonight. Okay, bye."

As Mina ended the call, she turned back to John, "Good call, making your son think you were dead somewhere."

149

John looked disappointed with himself, "I understand you're upset and you have good reason to be. I wanted you to be the first to know, as well as to ask for your help in telling the others." Mina took a deep breath and said, "I'm not telling them anything. You need to come clean to them yourself."

Mina began to walk away but stopped and said, "Also, it's too late for you to try to go back. There is an extra bed down here or there's the couch. But once the sun has gone down, I want you out."

"Understood," John said.

He rose from his seat and went over to the living room and closed the curtains. He went over to the small couch and got comfortable.

Mina went upstairs and got herself into bed. No need in getting changed since she had only worn the outfit for an hour or so. Laying in bed, something didn't sit right with John's truth, as if he was still not sharing the whole story. Why was it so important for him to keep the others in the dark about human blood? What was he planning?

She was asleep for maybe a few hours when she heard a door downstairs open up. Judging by the sound of the door, it was the backdoor. Was John trying to get back to camp? It was nowhere near time for the sun to go down.

Mina threw back her covers and ran downstairs without even thinking to bother with shoes.

When Mina reached the back porch, she saw John walking through the field. Thankfully there were large gray rain clouds in the sky, and what do you know, it began to rain.

"John!" Mina called after him but he did not reply to her. Mina had two choices, either catch up to him and get him quickly back to camp before the sun made its debut again, or, leave him to his decision of walking off before it was safe.

With that, she chose the first and went after him. She began to jog towards him but soon realised the rain was letting up. Mina looked at the sky and realized there was a break in the clouds that would let sunshine appear for a moment. Mina decided it was time to get John to the camp with all she had.

For the first time in centuries, Mina built up a good run and let her wings burst free from the flesh of her back as they tore through her shirt. Beating them against the air, she gained more speed and was in flight to John. She flew to him and scooped him up in the knick of time. The sunlight was on her like it was specifically chasing her, but Mina was too fast. She reached the tree line and then soon enough she was at the camp.

She set John down and looked at the sky. The sun had disappeared once more and the rain returned.

"WHAT THE FUCK WERE YOU THINKING?" Mina yelled, waking the whole camp with her booming voice.

"Were you trying to get yourself killed? Trying to make Sam an orphan so you didn't have to share your little secret?"

Mina didn't realize that at this point, everyone from the camp was standing around her in a circle, watching as she scolded their leader.

"You saved me..." John began to state, as if to show gratitude to keep on with his nice guy act.

"No, I kept you from making a stupid decision and abandoning these people."

Mina heard a voice speak up then that registered in her heart, it was Sam.

"Mina?"

She turned around quickly and saw the look upon his face, it was that of amazement. Mina hadn't realized that her wings were still on full display for all to see.

She began looking at the faces surrounding her and seemingly decided to panic. No one had ever seen her wings, not even her mother or maid. They had known her special gift, but never saw her in action with them. Mina was at her most vulnerable state while she stood frozen in the middle of the circle.

She took one more look at Sam and, since it was still raining, she took her chance to get home as quickly as possible. She put her wings straight to the sky and with a swift motion, pushed herself off the ground. Flying high above the trees, she could hear Sam calling after her, but she paid him no attention. She wanted to get back home so she could be alone for a while and decompress.

Landing on the lawn, she quickly got onto the porch and into her house. She closed and locked the door behind her so no one could follow her and get in.

As she made her way up to her room, she lost her balance and crashed to the floor. Mina felt overwhelmed by the amount of faces staring at her and her wings that she didn't know how to process her feelings. Laying there, she thought about what Sam might think of her now and if maybe she should just kill them all and leave to move somewhere new.

Mina spent hours debating things in her head and realized she was in complete darkness, "Night," she said.

Looking at her phone, she saw there were no texts and no missed calls from anyone. Were they scared of her? Was it because she was yelling at their 'wonderful' leader? The multiple questions ran through her head. 'I should have just let him burn up and then Sam could hate me and I could leave them all behind,' she thought to herself.

Then Mina heard footsteps arriving at her back porch, followed by a knock.

Seventeen

Sam had decided to stay at camp and allow Mina some alone time after she arrived earlier with his father. He wasn't sure exactly what she meant by his father's, 'little secret'.

Sam couldn't go back to sleep, but with the rain still falling, he could walk around camp without any risk. Sam went to his fathers side and knelt down beside him.

"Are you okay, dad?" Sam asked.

"I am. I'm very thankful Mina was able to get me back here and away from the sun," John replied.

"Dad, what were you doing by leaving her house in the middle of the day? Why didn't you just wait until nightfall?"

"I wanted to get back here as soon as I could. When I saw it began to rain, I figured I'd be okay."

"It wasn't worth the risk. But what did she mean by you having a secret?"

Sam grew frustrated as his father remained silent and didn't answer his question.

"Dad, Answer me." Sam pushed.

"Not here. Take me to my tent and I'll tell you everything."

Sam helped his father to his feet and accompanied him to his tent. Once they arrived, Sam followed his father in and watched as his father took a seat on his bed. Sam remained motionless, content with standing and awaiting whatever news he was about to hear.

"Well?" Sam said impatiently.

John told him the full story and then added why he chose to leave her house in the middle of the day.

"So you knew there was a chance you could have been killed and you left the house betting on it?"

"Yes. I couldn't come to terms with myself that I had turned all these people and they still weren't at complete status with their transition."

Sam couldn't even find the words to tell his father how he felt.

"Tonight, you will tell them all the truth and allow them to choose if they want the transition to be complete or not."

John fell silent again, but Sam continued, "And then you will apologize and leave. You are no longer welcome

here. If the others decide they want you to stay…. then I'll
be the one to leave."

"You will do no such thing. This is your home. Your
family."

"I have no family! These people you call family are
strangers that you took free will from. You took their
choice of life or death away from them."

"That is not what I did. I told you, I…"

Sam interrupted him, "You created them for me? No,
you created them for you. You did this so that way you
were in control and felt important. You did this for
yourself."

Sam saw the wheels in John's head begin to turn and
said, "Don't be a coward."

Sam left the tent and walked to the edge of the camp to
have some time to himself. It wasn't long before someone
decided to join him. Sam inhaled and could tell from some
scent he picked up on, that it was a female approaching.

"Not now Jessica." Sam said bluntly, "I'm not in the
mood to deal with you today."

"I'm not trying to start a fight, I only want to ask you
what is going on between her and your father", she asked
him while keeping her distance.

Since Sam completed his transition, people looked at
him differently and treated him with a sense of fear but
more respect. Being larger, he intimidated the males and

being stronger, he tempted the females. Yet, both kept their distance due to not knowing what he was now capable of.

"He will share with you what he has told me by tonight," he replied.

"Sam, I'm sorry for how I behaved at Mina's. I shouldn't have said those things. I do truly like you and thought for a second you liked me, too. But then she showed up and you weren't mine anymore."

"I was never yours, Jessica, and I really need you to understand that once and for all."

"I do. I fully understand that now."

"Good. Now, can you please leave me alone? Physically?"

She didn't say anything to him, just turned and walked back to the heart of camp.

'God, what Mina must be feeling,' Sam thought to himself after he saw the panic in her eyes. When he saw her wings, he was immediately infatuated with them. They were the most beautiful thing he has ever seen in his life and hoped she would allow him to see them again. But he wouldn't push her. Right now she needed space, but he would go to her once the sun had set.

Sam was all alone, staring into the abyss of trees that surrounded the camp. He had his thoughts for company, although all they could think of was getting to Mina.

After a few hours, Sam made the decision to make his way to his female.

Yes, he meant Mina and wasn't afraid to admit it, or make it known to the others. Sam walked through the middle of camp and others stared at him. Speaking low to others of the dramatic entrance that occurred earlier, Sam ignored them all. He was on a mission and damn anyone who got in his way.

After a short walk, he arrived at Mina's porch. No lights on, and no movement could be heard through the house. Not trying to panic, he calmly walked to the backdoor and knocked. With there being no answer and no sound of movement, he tried the doorknob. It was locked.

"Mina?" he asked with a regular voice, knowing well enough that she could hear him. "Mina, please. Open the door. It's just me, I want to see you," Sam said as reassuringly as he could. He wanted her to know she was safe and that nothing was going to happen to her.

With there still being no answer, he made the executive decision to climb up to where her bedroom window was. With his new found strength, this was an easy task and he kind of impressed himself with the action. He jumped up and grabbed the porch roof with his hands, pulled himself up and walked to the window.

He looked inside the dark room and could hear Mina's heartbeat loud and clear. 'She's in there,' he said to himself.

Sam tapped on the window to see if he could get some kind of reaction from her or movement. Still nothing.

As his last resort, he tried opening the window. It was stubborn at first and would not budge, but soon he heard a snap sound and the thing opened wide for him. He climbed in, shut the window and saw her there just laying on the floor. She seemed completely lifeless as he walked over to the floor where she was. Dropping his body down to her, he used his hand to push back some of her hair from her face and behind her ear.

"Mina? Can you sit up for me?" Sam asked. With no answer, he slid his arms under her and lifted her up to her bed and gently placed her down.

"You know, we keep having this routine where I lay you in bed and it still doesn't lead to me climbing in there with you," he joked, as if to make her smile or break whatever train of thought was occurring. Still, there was no reply and Sam was getting concerned.

"Mina, my Mina."

That got her to look at him at least. "Please, talk to me. Tell me what's wrong so that I can try and help you come back to the world."

She continued to look at him but then her eyes glanced behind her where her shirt had been torn from when her wings busted through.

"Oh," he said, "yes, I know. And they were beautiful. But it doesn't change the way I look at you. You are still the same head strong female I've gotten to know these past few months."

Those words had her pick her head up off the bed and look at him.

"How could you say that after seeing me?"

"Easily, because I just did."

He allowed her time to speak, and she said, "You are the only one to see me that way, ever."

Sam was shocked by this news and slightly honored. Although, it wasn't just him to see it, there were about ten other witnesses.

"I can't imagine what that must have been like for you. I'm so sorry that my father did what he did. He was a fool, and after what I found out today, I'm honestly okay with never seeing him again."

"So you know?" Mina asked

"Yes. But did he say why he came to you first?"

"He said he wanted me to tell them so he could still seem to be in the dark about this too and not be the bad guy."

"Mina, I hate that you got brought into this drama. I'm not sure what he was thinking when he took those peoples lives."

"He said it was for you, but I don't believe him."

"It wasn't for me, it was for him. Or, at least that's what I took away from his confession."

Mina stayed silent when Sam spoke again, "Would you do something for me?"

"Anything."

"Would you show me how to hunt humans? So that way I can also help the others if they decide to complete their change?"

"Of course. Give me a second and I'll get dressed. We can go tonight since I'm hungry and need to hunt."

Mina rose out of bed and began taking her clothes off. The shorts went into the hamper and the shirt into the trash.

Sam turned around so he could give her privacy, "Oh sorry, I'll go downstairs"

He began to walk but was stopped before he made it to the door. It was Mina's hand on his bicep.

"You don't have to go. I don't mind if you see me."

Sam turned around and saw her, every square inch of her body was exposed. His eyes looked her up and down and took all of her in. He watched her get dressed and never once looked away. He watched as she bent over to put on her jeans and watched her breasts move freely with the movements. She walked over to her closet and grabbed a bra, placing it around her and doing up the back before sliding the straps over her shoulders.

All he was thinking about was going primal on her and wanted to take her now. Sam had to refocus his thoughts and shift his pants a little before he was in real trouble. Mina must have noticed what he was doing because she commented, "Let's see how you do tonight, then maybe you can let him loose later."

Blushing at her comment, Sam felt like a teenage boy watching her as she dressed like that, but he felt absolutely mesmerized by her. She found a green shirt from her closet and put it on while heading for the stairs.

They made their way down the steps, out the front door and walked in silence. He was behind her, as a protector should be, even though he was well aware that she could take on twice more than he could. But his male instincts told him to stay behind so he could protect her anyway possible.

They walked until they reached the city limits of downtown Savannah.

"Okay, let's get started," said Mina.

<u>Eighteen</u>

"Sir? Can I get you anything?" the slender stewardess asked.

Dragos was high in the sky when the little black haired woman came by and asked her question. "No," he replied, "But perhaps, is there anything not on the menu that I could possibly indulge myself with?"

As the question was asked, the woman stood to her full height and gave him a 'you're disgusting' type of look before she walked back to the front of the jet.

'Eh, I tried,' he thought to himself. After being in a form of vampire coma for over 500 years, a man has needs. Dragos remembered back when he was doing missions for the king, he would always visit the local pubs for a 'sweet fix' before heading back to the castle.

Feeling confident, Dragos looked to the front and saw that black haired beauty sitting alone and not talking to anyone. He pressed his call button and the woman left her seat to see what he wanted. "Yes?" she asked with a tone.

"If you do not wish to talk to me, then perhaps there is another who would like to bring me a drink," he said.

"It's just me today, besides, of course, the pilot at the front."

"Ah, well I'd love some sort of beverage. Bring me whatever sounds good."

She walked off without a word, possibly a sigh of relief, and returned shortly with a short glass in hand. "Here you go. Is there anything else I can do for you?"

Dragos moved the glass in circles while he watched the brown liquid inside move around. Without looking up, he replied, "No, that is all."

As she began to walk away, Dragos moved so quickly there was no way for her to react. He scooped her up and took her closer to the back of the jet. Not that there was really much room to go anywhere.

Holding her facing away from him, Dragos kept her mouth covered and whispered, "Scream, and I'll kill you."

Nodding her head in acceptance of his terms, he lowered his hand to the collar of her shirt. Placing his mouth to her neck, he bit her. She gasped a little at the brief but abrupt pain at her neck, yet she didn't say a word.

Dragos took the same hand used to move her collar around and lowered it to the first button of her shirt. He slowly released each button until her tan bra was exposed. Not messing with the contraption on her chest, he slid his hand inside the right cup and found her nipple. Another gasp left the woman's mouth as he began rolling it around with his fingers. A little pleasure as a reward for her not screaming when his teeth punctured her skin.

While keeping contact with her neck and continuing to tease her, he slipped his other free hand to the hem of her skirt. Lifting it up, he made his way to the line of her panties and maneuvered his hand underneath.

When he had found his destination, the woman tried to throw herself forward from pleasure. She had no success due to his tight hold on her. While making circling motions with his fingers at her sex, she attempted to escape his grasp, yet was unsuccessful once again.

Once he got his fill in blood, he was ready to get his fill in another area. Removing his hands from her, he retracted his fangs and bent her over so she was holding on to the small sofa. "Please, dont...." He immediately shut her up by placing two of his large fingers back inside her. As he vigorously pulled them out and shoved them in, she became more and more wet for him.

When he had finished teasing her, he went to his pants and untied the piece of leather that kept them bound. Once untied, he slid his pants down a little and his massive cock sprung free from its cotton prison.

The woman looked over her shoulder to see what was coming for her and fear consumed her. Before she could scream, Dragos grabbed her by the throat and said, "If you want to keep your windpipe, you won't make a sound." He didn't release his hand from her, keeping his hand on her neck while his cock found its place.

Like a key sliding into a lock, he wasted no time as he thrust all of himself into her until he could go no further. She inhaled sharply from the pain she felt as he forced her body to expand and accept his size. He began to pump quickly as if he had a time limit or was in a race. While inside her, he felt her cum so aggressively that she shook from head to toe. She tried to push away from him to escape his grasp but he wouldn't let her move an inch. Shortly thereafter it was his turn and he came inside her.

Releasing himself once wasn't enough to satiate him. Just as she sighed a breath of relief, he began again with the thrusting motions. Except this time, he flipped her over and ripped her bra off so he could watch her breasts move with him. He came twice more after his first release, and the woman could barely breathe. She looked as if she had been through war.

Dragos didn't care, though. He was satisfied and went back to his seat, not paying any attention to the woman crying as she made her way to the jet's restroom. He was a cold hearted male who only took for his own benefit.

After what seemed like an hour or so, he heard the woman emerge from the bathroom and make her way back to her seat at the front. She had a stain from him on the back of her skirt and he could tell she was no longer wearing her bra, since he had been the one to destroy it. He took the vision of her defeat as his own personal victory.

Dragos accepted the fact he was a monster and took pride in bringing harm to others. That was why he was chosen and raised to be the king's hand. Death and torture? Such simple tasks for him to complete.

For the remaining duration of the trip, he spent his time looking out the window and eye fucking the woman at the front. Mind games were so much fun and torturing her was bringing him a sense of joy he hadn't felt in a long time.

The flight still had a remaining eight hours to go before they reached their destination. Dragos had an idea of how to spend his time but he could tell that the woman wouldn't come close to him again. Which was fine, he instead began looking at a paper map that the council members had supplied him with and began getting a lay of the land. He wanted to make sure he knew where he was going once they landed and he could immediately find the princess.

Nineteen

Savannah was beautiful at night as the street lights illuminated the city and made it seem like something out of a Hallmark movie. It was late summer and there were plenty of humans out at night, still spending their paycheck on drinks and living like tomorrow will never come.

Sam missed that part of life, not that he really went out with people, but having so much fun you would forget your problems. Now? Tomorrow is the same as yesterday without any end in sight.

Sam followed Mina through the main part of downtown Savannah and they blended right in with the crowd of humans. "Want a drink?" Mina shouted over the crowd. "Sure!" Sam yelled back.

The music surrounded them as they made their way into a bar and ordered some drinks. Mina handed the bartender a $20 and got them a couple beers to enjoy. Once they received their beverages from the guy, they walked back out into the open air. They found an open table and sat down.

"So, since you have been around for like.... ever. Have you been here before?" Same asked.

"I have. It was back in the 20's and this place was a speakeasy. There is a special cellar below that people would gather to drink in. Unless someone filled it in or blocked it off in some way."

"We should go see if it's still here," Sam tempted.

"Okay!" Mina said enthusiastically. She was in the mood for a little adventure and kind of liked seeing Sam light up like that.

They finished their beers and left the empty brown bottles at the table. Going back inside, Mina went to the back where the bathrooms were. She began feeling the wall and felt a slight divot in the current wallpaper that had been placed. "This is the entrance," she said, "but it seems like they covered it up so no one can go down there anymore."

Mina grabbed Sam by the hand and led him back outside and around to the back of the building. She began feeling for something. When she got to the right spot, the wall began to give to her weight.

"This was the 'emergency' exit- a special door where we could get out if we were ever found by the police." Mina shoved her weight a little more and the door opened up.

The empty space was like that of a horror movie. Cobwebs everywhere and broken wood from tables laid on the ground. Some of the chairs were still intact. "No Way!" Mina said as she ran further into the dark room. "This is the bar!"

Mina stood at a wooden counter type structure that was covered in dust and what seemed like rat poop. Sam tried to imagine what it was like all those years ago and what Mina may have looked like as a possible flapper girl.

"No, I wasn't a flapper. But I did wear similar things." Mina said as if answering his thought. "I would always sit over here as the man I was seeing bought me drink after drink," she continued, "His name was Henry and he was an old bastard who just wanted me as arm candy to show off to his friends. And, of course, make his wife jealous."

Sam tried not making a face that showed his disapproval when she talked of another man being by her side. Not that he was even around back then, but he definitely wasn't wanting to think of her with anyone but himself.

Mina walked over to one of the outside walls and placed a couple fingers up to a hole. "There was a man one night who was trying to cheat his way through a game of poker. Charles, I believe was his name. He ended up getting shot by his opponent who didn't care much for men with such low morals."

171

He was so amused watching her walk about the abandoned room and hear her stories from the time she would visit the place. They both agreed they were ready to leave and Sam shut things up behind them once they were back outside.

"Do you miss it? That life from the 20's?" he asked.

"Not particularly. It wasn't a lifestyle I chose, but a lifestyle I had to live in order to blend in."

Walking away from the memory, Sam decided to take Mina's hand in his and was surprised she didn't protest to it. Seeming like an ordinary couple, they walked down a quiet street, away from the noise of the crowd.

"Okay, first, you don't want to draw attention to yourself."

'What? Oh, right. The hunting lesson,' Sam thought to himself, almost forgetting the main reason they came to town tonight.

Sam followed Mina's lead and went down a small alley between two businesses and ducked into the shadows.

"This seems a bit obvious. Who in their right mind is going to come down a...." Sam was cut short when he saw a homeless man sit against the alley wall at the opening. "I'm not killing a homeless man," he said firmly.

"Sam, use your senses. Smell for his blood and listen to his heart rate. He is old and dying anyway. His blood is not pumping as quickly as it should. Which means he is most likely going to die of some heart issue instead of old age or starvation."

Doing as she said, Sam opened his nose for the scent and focused on his hearing. He heard exactly what she was talking about and understood why she was making this man a target.

"Watch me."

Sam watched and she walked over to the man. He looked at her with kindness in his eyes and she said something to the man but he wasn't paying attention to that. With a subtle but kind movement, Mina went to the man's throat and began to feed. It wasn't any more than a minute later, Mina placed the man's collar up so it would cover the puncture wounds and she rose to her full height.

"So, he just let you feed on him?" Sam inquired.

"I asked what his disease was and he told me COPD. I then asked if he wanted an out so he didn't have to suffer. He agreed and I told him he would no longer feel any pain."

Sam was dumbfounded by how she took care of her victim and the fact that she made sure the man didn't feel anything. "It doesn't have to be dramatic or aggressive. The hunting I mean. It can seem like an act of kindness for some," Mina said, which brought Sam's attention back to her and not the now deceased man.

"So, when is it necessary to kill like they do in the movies?" Sam inquired.

Mina's laugh caught him off guard. "Never. The movies have it all wrong. Except that Dracula movie. They got close to the truth of our lifestyle." She continued to educate him, "I get crafty when it comes to the bad ones. The ones who commit a crime, beat the innocent or mistreat animals."

As if right on cue, the sounds of a man and a woman arguing in a park nearby came to their attention. Sam used his vampiric hearing to listen in on the conversation. It seemed like the man was upset that his woman found him cheating on her with her sister. 'Asshole', he thought to himself. As if Mina heard the same thing and knew that was what Sam was going to go after, she jogged behind him until he reached the large park.

"Quit crying, bitch! It's your fault I cheated on you! You aren't as hot as her!" shouted the man to the woman.

Sam rolled his eyes as his anger roared inside him. No woman deserves that, human or vampire.

Before Sam could make his move, Mina grabbed his arm to stop him.

"Not him" she said, "he cheated. He's a piece of shit, but doesn't deserve to die over it."

"So how do we know who does and doesn't? I'm not trying to play God," Sam argued.

"We're not. But you need to be wise about who you go after. Keep looking for the right target."

Sam and Mina continued walking, coming across too many people who fell into the category of your average drunk person or someone who probably took too many drugs. But no one was standing out to Sam as a possible target.

About a mile away, Sam heard a woman crying. Picking up a light jog, he ran over to a part of town that wasn't filled with as many 'good vibes' as downtown was. The roads were poorly lit, yet Sam could see perfectly fine. Off to the right of where they were standing was a woman who didn't seem to be having such a good time with her guy friend. He had her pinned up against a wall with a knife to her neck.

"If you scream one more fucking time, Ill open you wide up!" the man threatened.

Sam could smell the fear radiating off the woman as if it were a perfume. Looking over at Mina for some validation, she nodded at him slightly in a non-verbal agreement. Sam used his training and stalked his prey from some trees that were lined up near where the humans were standing. He knew he wanted to be smart, but not take up too much time.

Sam moved quickly and grabbed the man from behind, without injuring the woman in any way, pulling him back into the trees. Sam held the man in place and kept him silent while the woman fled.

Sam wasted no time with talking, the words wouldn't matter once the man was dead. Following through, Sam bit the male and drained him of everything he had. As soon as the man went limp and it was becoming harder and harder for Sam to pull blood, he dropped the body and left him to rot. Before he walked away, he grabbed a stick from one of the trees and jammed it into the guy's neck so no puncture wounds would be found. He walked proudly over to Mina and she had a look of pride on her face.

"Well done! I believe you are ready to graduate," she said

They both laughed and began to walk back towards downtown to head home. Along the way, she informed him that you don't or shouldn't kill more than one human every few days or so, just so people don't panic about a serial killer or anything.

With the human blood in his stomach, Sam's hunger was satisfied. Yet another kind of hunger was lingering around inside, just waiting to be fed.

Mina was walking in front of him and he couldn't help but look at her ass and how her hips swayed gently from side to side.

They agreed that they had enough fun for the night and began their journey back to the farmhouse. But something felt off, something in the air felt different.

****

Mina was thinking about how well Sam had done tonight and how he took to it a lot better than she had expected him to. She could feel his eyes on her as she walked and was purposely walking with a big more swing in her hips just for him.

The air got thicker as they got closer and closer to the farmhouse and she knew exactly what was going to happen. They fed, but Sam wasn't even close to being done with hunting. Feeling like there was a dog behind her, Mina could hear the low hungry growl in Sam's chest. Mina was ready for him and almost expected him to not be so gentleman-like when they arrived home.

They arrived back on the property an hour or so before the sun was set to rise. Walking up the porch, Mina turned to look at Sam, and he was right on her heels.

"So, the sun will be here soon, and I'm sure you want to get back to the camp to see your dad. Right?" she said, taunting him.

"No." he said as he used his body to push her inside. But she was much stronger than him.

"Fine." Sam said as he grabbed her by the throat and slammed her up against the side of the house.

They shared a look of hunger for one another and Sam took that as some sort of green light. He took his other hand and pulled her top down to where her bra was. Without wasting any time or waiting for her to protest, he pulled one of the soft cups to the side and released her breast.

Sam dipped his head down and began sucking on her tight hard nipple. Playing with it, teasing her, he eventually brought his head back up and slid everything back into place.

Yet she stood still and didn't move a muscle.

"Mina, I'm not to be played with. Now let me inside," he demanded.

'Okay, that's sexy,' she said in her head. Deciding to toy with him a little longer, she backed away quickly and shut the door in his face. She didn't lock it, but was glad he got the hint to wait.

Mina watched as her male gazed at her like prey he was going to consume. She teased him by slowly and fully removing her top and bra, completely exposing herself to him. Continuing on, she went to the button of her jeans and undid them so she could slide them off. She had matching black panties on that were sheer enough to almost be see through.

As she stood there nearly naked, she could hear his heart pounding and his breathing increase as he stared at her with those demanding eyes.

To finish off his patience, she removed her panties, and revealed what he had been wanting most. Sam was about to break her door down if he couldn't get to her, which he could but he waited like a good boy for her to signal she was ready for him.

Mina turned so he could see her bare ass and began to walk away. That's when she heard the door burst open like an explosion. Sam came from behind her more quickly than she had ever witnessed him move. He grabbed her around the waist and football carried her up the stairs. He was done waiting and she was ready for him to have her.

Reaching her room, Sam immediately began where he left off the other night. He pushed her against the wall and didn't wait for permission before using his hand to find her sex. She didn't panic, letting Sam do what he wanted. And wanting it, too, she was happy to let him.

She began to breathe harder as he teased her insides with his fingers and used his mouth to play with one of her nipples. While he was sucking and pulling at her she looked down at him to watch. The sight of him was enough to make her cum all together. But she wasn't ready for that... yet.

She wanted to have some fun, too. Using her strength, she used her hand to grab at Sam. She quickly found something to hold onto that was rock hard and ready to be used. She just needed to release it from its hiding place in his pants.

She pushed him back and he hit the opposite wall from where they had started. Without wasting any time, Mina ripped his shirt off.

"Damn," she expressed as she looked at his rock hard body. There was no time to gawk as she continued onto those stupid pants that were in the way. She pulled them off him with ease, especially since he wasn't wearing a belt.

When she pulled them off, his boxers came off with them and his thick length nearly hit her in the face.

Sam threw back his head with ecstasy and looked back down at Mina.

She grabbed him with her hand and began stroking him, gaining more speed and then stopped. She placed him in her mouth and started sucking at him. Using her tongue to trace the side of his cock, she teased him a little. That got him even more hard, although it seemed impossible at that point.

She continued to use her tongue to play with his head and next thing she knew, she was lifted off the floor and thrown onto the bed.

He chose to have her facing him, and he threw her legs over his shoulders, basically having a staring contest with her wet sex. Mina jumped when he began to lick her from back to front, taking his time as he passed over her most sensitive spot.

With no shame, he wanted to taste her. He sucked on her clit and used his tongue to flick at it. Mina tried to push him away to escape the intensity of the pleasure, but he kept pulling her back. He was nowhere near done with her and he wasn't going to let her get away this time.

Mina came so intensely that she convulsed like she was having a seizure. Sam gave her no time to think before pulling back and bringing his mouth to hers. She was breathing hard as he went to her neck and began biting and sucking at it while he used his hand to play with her nipple.

She grabbed him by the hair and pulled his head back.

"Fuck me." she said, demanding him.

He didn't answer, just climbed up on the bed and opened her up, with her legs falling to either side. He positioned himself at her opening and slid right in. Mina cussed with pleasure as he came immediately. She felt every gush that came from him, but he continued to fuck her, just as she told him to do.

They made eye contact and she watched as his body moved with his hips while he slid in and out. He had a devilish smile on his face as he flipped her over without breaking them apart. This time, they came together. Sam fell off her and onto the bed beside her. Mina remained on her stomach while she tried to recover her breathing to a normal rate.

"Fuck." she heard him say, "That.... Was ..... Great," he said between breaths.

"See? Human blood. Worth it." Mina panted.

After laying on the bed for a few minutes, Mina sat up and lowered her feet to the hardwood floor.

"You want water?" she asked Sam.

"No, I want you to get that ass back in bed."

Mina giggled like a school girl at how cute Sam was being. She didn't understand why he was so different from the rest, but he was and she accepted that anyway. She climbed back into bed and they fell asleep just as the sun reached its highest point in the sky. This was the happiest she had been in a while, and hoped it wasn't going to end.

Twenty

John had been sitting alone in his tent since Sam left to go after Mina. He sat quietly and pondered his thoughts about 'completing the transition'. He debated with himself if he should go ahead and complete it or keep to his word about being 100% human-free vampires. His biggest fear was that, if he told everyone the truth, they would want to go off on their own or have Sam as their leader. Not that he cared if they wanted to go, but he didn't want them to choose his son over him.

John always had problems being the one to follow directions and would rather be the one giving them. Before he turned and long before he got sick, John was a supervisor for a shipping company. He was the one giving orders, telling people where they needed to be and what their duties were for that day.

Unbeknownst to him, there was another man who was trying to take John's position. When John found out, he planted a worm in people's ear about the other man and got him fired. John didn't mess around when it came to being in control. He would be nice to them and get them to feel sorry about situations he was in that may or may not have been completely true. He controlled people by using them and manipulating them into being his 'friend'.

It wasn't long after John turned that he began finding people and turning them, just to turn around and be their savior with this 'vampire camp' that he came up with. He had his followers and told them a lie that would prevent them from leaving.

His internal battle now consisted of whether he should go against his own word, or stay by it.

As the sun set and the night sky appeared above him, John emerged from his tent and walked away from the camp. He said hello to fellow campers, just as he did any other day. But he did not sit for breakfast. Instead, he continued walking through the woods.

Somewhere not too far in front of him, he heard someone talking, then he smelled smoke. A small campsite came into his view and he saw a man sitting at the fire talking into a camera. 'This is it,' John thought to himself. Finding a log to sit on, John got comfortable in the shadows and watched as the man ate his dinner with his virtual audience and waited for the man to turn the camera off.

An hour went by and the man finally shut things down and put his fire out. John walked up to the man's camp and opened his tent. The man said nothing and just looked at John with fear. John couldn't move very quickly due to his gimp leg, but he did what he had to so he could kill the human and take what was needed for him to become like Sam.

Doing what he considered the typical vampire thing and going for the neck, he didn't really aim for the carotid artery, he just threw himself at the man and bit down.

The strong taste of pennies from the iron in the man's blood hit John's tongue and he became immediately addicted. With every pull, he wanted more and more. It was a slow flow due to him not hitting the human's carotid, but it still got the job done.

Once finished, John let the man's lifeless body fall back and he just stared at the human. "That wasn't so bad," John said to himself.

He felt his body begin to change, pains disappeared and his limp was gone. He could feel himself breathe better and he felt as if he could lift a car.

John began to walk back through the woods and he felt sixty years younger. He even picked up a good jog and discovered that he was much faster than he was as an animal-only vampire.

Approaching the camp, he stopped in his tracks and crouched down in the weeds. He thought about what his next move should be and the possible consequences. He saw a woman walking to the garden behind the camp and she began harvesting vegetables. She saw John and waved to him as if it were any other day.

As John rose to his feet, her face changed from happiness to concern and then to fear. It was so strong he could smell the fear on her like a deer to a hunter. She turned to get someone for help but he was too fast. He came up on her and snapped her neck. She wasn't dead yet, but he moved her body to a spot where the sun would get her.

He wasn't bothered by her dying because of him, which would concern most people, but just continued on into the camp. Somehow he made his way back into his tent without being seen. Everyone was most likely busy with their daily tasks before it was time to turn in.

He paced back and forth inside and thought about his next move. His heightened senses included heightened emotions, which meant his anger towards Mina was at its peak. "It all began with her," he said to himself, "she came here and changed Sam and changed the way he thought. Sam was just fine as he was. I made the choice to let her into our home. But how can I get rid of her?"

John continued to pace and ask himself questions to try to figure out how to solve his problems. He stopped and realized that he had spent hours in his tent and missed dinner. He could hear the clinking of plates and the running water used to wash the dishes.

"John? Are you there?" questioned Dom from outside the tent.

"Yes, but I am tired and am going to bed. I'll see everyone tonight."

He listened as he heard Dom walk off without another word. John laid down and figured out another plan, in which he vocalised to himself, "Mina must go. And if my son will not stand with me, then he must go as well."

It wasn't long after his self-proclaimed declaration of war that he decided to rest in preparation of what the next night would bring. He didn't want to waste any time with the punishment he had planned in his head.

****

Mina woke up next to the large male she had let into her bed, into her life and well, into her. She was facing him and looked at his face while he continued sleeping. He was so beautiful, even though he wasn't a full born vampire. But now his features were much more defined. As she finished giving her male a look over, she slid out of the bed quietly and went over to the bathroom. She and Sam had never dressed after their little 'adventure', so when she got to the bathroom she chose to run a hot bath. Turning the water on, she saw it was still daylight, but knew she wouldn't mind crawling back into bed with Sam once her bath was finished.

Getting into the hot water, she started with her hair and used the handheld shower head to rinse out the shampoo and conditioner. Then she chose to relax for a moment and take in everything that happened last night/this morning.

Sam was a good hunter and it came to him naturally. Mina felt like a proud teacher and smiled at the fact that he went after someone being mean to a woman. Then her mind traveled to when they arrived back home and the details of how they both ended up naked and in bed. She had a large smile on her face from the memory and she used the bottle of generic body wash to wash her body with a washcloth. She missed her Bath and Body Works products but there wasn't one near her that she could easily go to.

As she sat in the soapy water, off in the distance, Mina heard a voice again.

'Mina'

Mina immediately sat up in the bath and cautiously looked out the window. But there was no one to be seen.

'Ugh, not again.' She thought to herself. It had been months since she heard the indiscernible voice. She figured that after the dream she had about Dimitri, that it was gone for good.

'Mina' came the voice once more, but this time it sounded a bit closer.

As Mina began to stand up and look for a towel, she heard movement coming from her room. 'Must be Sam woke up,' she thought. Just as the thought came to her, Sam came through the bathroom door with concern plastered on his face. Mina looked up at him as she was just about to step out of her bath.

"I hope I didn't wake you, I...." Mina said as her words began to trail off.

She took in his body with her eyes as they traveled down to that length between his legs. Even when he wasn't hard, it was still a sight to see. "Um, I figured I'd take a quick bath before you got up," she finished as her eyes made their way back up to his face.

"You should have woke me, I would have joined you," he replied.

"Have you noticed how large you have become since you fully turned? Like all of you grew. We both wouldn't fit."

He smirked as he said, "I mean, you're not wrong. I have grown in more ways than my height. But there is an easy solution to the 'party for two' problem in the tub."

He walked towards her with purpose and was now face to face with her. "I could sit down, and then you could straddle my lap while I bathe you."

Mina was at a loss for words. She blushed and before she could think of it, Sam scooped her up and stepped into the bath himself. Not caring about the fact that she was already clean, he lowered her back onto her feet while he sat down. He then grabbed her by the ass and pulled down to motion her to lower down to him.

Mina did exactly as Sam moved her with no protest. She placed one foot on either side of him and lowered herself down into the water. What she found was her sex reaching something hard sticking up in the water. Sam moved his hips slightly and next thing she knew, she was on him.

Thankfully, vampires aren't prone to the same issues humans are. So she didn't have to worry about some infection from the soapy water getting in her.

As she took all of him in, she grabbed onto his shoulders and pulled him into her. His mouth found her nipple once more and began sucking and teasing it with his tongue, like his life depended on it.

Mina couldn't help but let out a loud moan from the contact he made with his mouth, and she began to roll her hips in a circular motion. Sam had no choice but to release his mouth from her and lean back to let her ride him more freely.

The water began to splash around them as she worked her hips against his, but nothing left the tub. It wasn't long until they both finished at the same time and Mina found herself throwing her body forward onto his.

They both sat still against each other while their breathing continued to labor on. Once Mina caught her breath, she leaned back and just looked at him. He stared back at her with nothing but admiration in his eyes. He took his hand and cupped her face and stroked her cheek with his thumb. They were officially and undeniably in love with each other. She was his and he was hers.

The happy couple emerged from the bath with Sam picking her up and not letting her feet touch the ground. Once back into the bedroom, he placed her down on her feet and found a towel, which he used to dry her off and then himself. Mina saw the trail of water they left behind and commented, "You may want to clean that up, too. Can't have these old floors getting damaged."

He nodded in agreement and walked his naked self back towards the bathroom, using his foot to swipe the towel back and forth to get the water droplets. When he returned Mina was already in the process of getting dressed. She could feel his eyes on her but she continued anyway. Just as she was sliding in her jeans,

'Mina'

Hearing the whisper, she shot up straight and looked at Sam.

"What? What is it?" Sam asked.

"I, um, did you hear that?" Sam looked at her with a look like she was crazy and replied, "Hear what?"

"That whisper. It keeps saying my name but I don't know who or what it is." Sam walked over to her and pulled her in, noticing she was slightly on edge about it.

"When did you start hearing it?"

"When I left Chicago, it was right before I arrived here in Savannah. Then, again, just before I reached the farmhouse for the first time." Mina continued telling Sam the times she has heard it. She even went into detail of the dream she had of Dimitri.

"It sounds like the whisper pops up when something is about to happen," Sam suggested as he held her to his chest.... and his still naked body.

"So, then, what is about to happen?" she asked him.

"I'm not sure, but at least we can plan to expect something."

Mina pulled away from him and finished getting dressed. All she had left was her bra, shirt and socks. Sam followed her lead and put his own clothes back on.

"There is one thing we should probably do before anything else tonight," Mina stated. Sam raised an eyebrow at her in confusion.

"We need to take care of that woman's body from the other night." It had been a couple days since Sam took the woman's life to save his own. Chances are her body was already decomposing, but if her A/C was on, she may not be too bad.

Mina looked outside and saw the sun had set and the sky was growing darker. She and Sam left the house and began their trek to the little red cottage a few miles up the road. He didn't walk next to her again, but continued behind her. She never would have thought that she would feel more safe with a male at her back than alone.

Twenty One

Dragos landed at his destination and made his way to the private arrival area. Inside he was greeted by a man who thanked him for flying with them.

"Where can I get some clothes?" asked Dragos.

"If you wish to shop within the airport, there is a store upstairs that would have some things for you."

Deciding he could use a change of wardrobe, he walked up the steps and found some pants and a crew neck t-shirt, both in black. After he paid for the clothes with some of the cash the council members gave him, he walked to the store next door and found a pair of boots that seemed less conspicuous than the ones he currently had on. He purchased them as well and went back to his waiting area. Dragos saw that the sun was rising and realized he was stuck indoors until it was safe.

Having nothing else to do, he decided it was as good a time as any to put on his new clothes. What Dragos didn't realize was that it wasn't a 100% private waiting area, and he was now joined by an older couple who had come in while he was gone. He began removing his clothing and heard a man clear his throat.

"Excuse me, but would you mind? This is not a locker room. Go change in the bathroom."

Dragos looked over his shoulder and saw the man sitting next to his wife, who was watching him intently and did not appear to be the least bit upset at the current live entertainment.

He ignored the man and continued on while he heard the human huff and puff. Dragos really threw things into a twist when he removed his pants to reveal he was wearing, well, no underwear. The woman gasped at the sight of him when he chose to turn around and really provoke the man.

The woman got red in her wrinkled face and the man was about to have a stroke from his anger. Dragos met her eyes and gave her a wink before putting on the new black jeans he had just purchased. Next was the shirt and then the boots. Everything fit well enough but didn't feel he had as much freedom to move as he did with his clothes from the 16th century.

Hours passed as he sat in the small waiting area with the older couple. Before he knew it, the sun was beginning to go down. He rose to his full height and walked toward the sliding glass doors. He passed by the older couple and winked once more at the woman, mainly to make her husband upset, but also to watch her blush like a schoolgirl.

Once he reached the outdoors, he began his walk in the direction the map showed. It seemed like the princesses address was roughly 250 miles from the Atlanta airport. Not a problem, Dragos was used to long treks across land. And just like that, he began his journey through the new land and kept focused on his goal. The princess.

As he walked, Dragos kept to the shadows as much as he could. He didn't want any humans to ask what he was doing or cause him any delay. Although he was used to a strictly human diet, he chose to err on the side of caution and feed on animals instead while he adjusted to this new era. At least he was lucky enough to find some form of shelter, just in time to get out of the sun each day. He continued walking, rain or shine, no matter the obstacle. Nothing was ever too much for him to handle.

Twenty Two

Sam and Mina walked up to the little cottage and could immediately smell the corpse waiting for them inside. Sam reached for the doorknob and walked in, where he was immediately greeted by a collection of snowglobes and china dishes. It somewhat reminded him of his grandmother's house before she had passed when he was little.

The kitchen was small with light blue walls and the living room had floral wallpaper. To the left of the doorway was a small eating area which still had a plate and silverware with crumbs. 'She must have just finished dinner,' he thought to himself.

Mina followed behind him and said, "Wow, this place has a lot of junk in it."

"It's not junk, more like nicknacks. Old women love to collect little things and place them around their house."

"Huh, odd." Mina replied.

Together they walked up the carpeted stairs and went
to the room where the smell was its strongest. Sam was the
first to enter and saw the woman in the same place he left
her. Laying in bed, eyes wide open in horror and two small
puncture marks at her neck.

"Damn," Mina said.

"We should bury her. It's the only way I won't feel so
guilty for killing her."

"Okay, sounds good to me." Mina picked up the old
woman with the quilt that was laid across her. Sam went
ahead of her to open doors and such, then went to the shed
to find a shovel. He found what he needed and began to
dig. He dug a 6ft hole about 20 feet away from the house
and they set her inside. He covered her up with the loose
dirt and stood in silence for a minute.

"Well, I suppose now I don't have to worry about being
evicted, " Mina said from behind him.

He looked at her lost, "What?" he asked.

"Oh, yeah. She was the woman who let me rent the
farmhouse. She was nice the day I met her but she didn't
have much longer to live anyway, maybe a year or so with
how that heart of hers was."

Sam was taken by Mina's words, they were empty and
had no remorse.

"She was still someone who I killed, and took that last little time away from her." Sam began to feel upset and he didn't even know her.

"Sam, I understand how you feel. After watching death come for people over and over for 500 plus years, I've learned to become detached. I'm not meaning to be heartless, it's just how I've come to terms with it."

Sam turned to her and said, "No, I get it. I'm just not as used to it as you are. At least we buried her. That part makes me feel slightly at peace."

Mina took his hand and led him away from the unmarked grave.

Sam stopped her, "Wait", he said abruptly.

"What?"

"Something isn't right," Sam said. He could feel the hairs on his arms and neck begin to stand, as if there was a storm coming.

For no reason, or a reason Sam didn't know yet, Mina took off at a dead run.

"Mina! Wait!" Sam called after her as he chased after her.

He watched as he saw Mina stop immediately in her tracks.

Sam caught up to her but instead of staying behind her, he put himself between her and whatever threat was coming their way. Getting into a 'I'm going to attack' stance, he heard Mina ask, "Sam? What do you sense?"

He ignored her so he could focus. It was a feeling he had never felt before. All he knew was that he was willing to die to protect his female. Even if she was stronger and faster than him. As a male, his instincts were to never allow a female to fight for you. It was an instinct he had before he turned, but now it was heightened.

Sam continued monitoring the area and soon realized what it was he was sensing.

****

Mina wasn't sure why she heard the whisper, or why it came from the direction of the farmhouse. But her gut told her to get back immediately.

Sam was in front of her, like a lion waiting to kill an unseen threat. She chose to help Sam by using her hearing yet she heard nothing. She picked up on some footsteps and that's when she could feel the aggression radiating off Sam.

"Sam?" she said, "Who is it?"

"My father."

Confused, she walked around him and asked, "Your father? Why are you in attack mode over him?"

Mina looked back into the field and saw why. His father no longer had a limp and he was larger. Mina came to the realization that he had completed his transformation.

"Sam, let me handle him. I can't let you get hurt."

"No, this is between me and him. I can take him."

Rather than argue, Sam began to run towards the back porch so he could get Mina inside and out of the line of fire.

"Get inside," he demanded, "Now."

"Sam, I'm stronger, let me...." He cut her off by turning and looking at her.

His eyes were dark and serious, which told her to let him do this.

Something inside her told her to let her male go and be the hero, to stay back. And she did. Mina backed up onto the porch but before she went inside, she saw that his father was not alone.

"Who is that with him?" Mina asked.

No answer came from Sam, then she saw who it was. Mina threw her hand up to cover her mouth as she saw that the now full vampire John had Dominic in his grasp. Dragging him along by the neck of his shirt.

Dominic wasn't necessarily a friend to her. He was pleasant, but her shock and anger was for Sam. That was Sam's best, and really only, friend.

John covered more and more ground with how quick he was walking. Mina went inside and let Sam have his time to stand up against his father.

"Let him go!" Sam demanded his father.

"Not yet. Give me Mina and you can have your little friend". Sam would never hand Mina over, even though he knew that if he did, she would kill him immediately with no struggle.

Mina listened to the banter between Sam and John, but didn't want to be sidelined for the whole fight. She wanted a small piece of action as well. But she let Sam take the reins on this one, unless he asked her to help.

She missed part of the conversation as she tried to think of some options they may have and before her eyes. Then John did the unforgivable.

****

Sam dropped to his knees as his friend's cry for help came to an abrupt silence. With one swift motion made by his father, he watched as his friend's head and body were separated. Sam could feel his blood begin to boil and decided that his father will die tonight.

Sam rose to his feet and his fangs extended to their full length. He began to run at his father, and his father stood still, awaiting the blow to come. Sam ran full force, but at the last minute quickly got behind his father and latched his fangs into his neck. Hands grabbed him and yanked him forward, breaking the contact from his fathers skin.

That began the punching, the biting and the scratching. It was a full on alpha versus alpha kind of fight. Each male was becoming more bloodied after each landed blow after blow on the other.

Not too long after the fight began, it was slowing down. John seemed to be out of moves and Sam was done with the nonsense all together. Sam landed a shot at his fathers knee, and the male collapsed. The older male dropped to the ground, howling with pain.

Sam took a moment to look over at Mina to make sure she was okay. Even though he knew for a fact she was, he just wanted the visual reassurance. Yet, Sam just broke one of the most important rules Mina had taught him in his training.

Seemingly fighting through the pain, John stood and got Sam in a vice grip as a last effort choke hold, which cut off Sam's air supply. Sam's world became darker and darker. Before he blacked out, he heard the beating of wings.

Twenty Three

Mina watched from her backdoor window as the two males fought it out. It took everything in her not to disobey Sam and go end things once and for all. Mina watched as they each took turns delivering and taking hits. Then she saw Sam take his father down.

"Yes!" she cheered out loud.

But in one swift movement, Sam was the one on the ground with John and gasping for whatever air he could inhale. John had his arm around Sam's airway and was squeezing as tight as he could.

'Okay, that's enough,' Mina thought to herself. She had finally claimed a male of her own and would be damned if she allowed him to be taken away so quickly.

Mina threw the backdoor open and took flight. Her wings beating as fast as they could to carry her to where the males were laying. Mina saw that Sam had lost consciousness, which was in a way a good thing for what she had planned for John.

"Wait," John said as he threw up his hands, "I'll leave. You can have him and everyone else at the camp. I don't want them."

Mina grabbed John by his throat and easily lifted him off the ground. She flew up into the air until they were as high as the top of the Empire State building.

When she reached her desired altitude, she looked at John's expression. It held nothing but fear.

"P-p-please! Don't do this, I didn't mean to cause harm!" John begged.

"No, you don't get to come here and do what you want without there being a consequence."

"Please, don't." John said as he held onto the hand that was holding him.

"Oh, don't worry, this won't kill you." That was when Mina let go of John and he started to fall. She stayed high above and watched as he plummeted to the ground below.

But, no, she wasn't done with him. Mina flew down to where John was still free falling, grabbing hold of him once more, but not stopping the fall. Instead she held on and flew him faster to the earth. When the impact was to occur, Mina pushed John into the ground, which created a divet in the dirt and grass from where his body slid.

Mina rose up with no problem, but John on the other hand was paralyzed. Mostly it was fear, but also because, even though he was a vampire, his spine had broken in every possible way.

Mina took to her darker side and tortured the male by removing parts that wouldn't heal until John wished for death. She did not take it lightly when her loved ones were attacked.

Soon after, John was dead.

Mina had his blood on her face and hands as she jogged back over to Sam.

Sam was still breathing, but was unconscious. It looked as if he was taking a nap. "I told you in training silly…. Don't take your eyes off the enemy." She could make light of it because she knew he was okay.

She didn't move him, just sat in the grass with her legs crossed. It wasn't long until he regained consciousness and his eyelids flew open.

"Mina, oh my Mina, are you okay?" Sam said quickly, making sure his father hadn't hurt her. "Why are you covered in blood?" he asked.

"It's your father's. I couldn't stay inside and let him think he won the fight. Let's just say he will never hurt you nor anyone else again."

She could see Sam's eyes flash a frustrated, 'I told you to stay inside' look but it quickly faded once he knew that his father was gone and she was okay.

That's when she looked to her right at the headless vampire still laying in the field. "We can bury him here at the farmhouse. I don't think I'm going anywhere anytime soon."

Sam nodded in agreement and they got to work laying his dear friend to rest.

Mina had a feeling that this wasn't that last time they would have to face danger. But she had hoped that it would be a little while before the next round showed up, whoever it may be.

Once she and Sam buried Dominic, she took Sam inside and had him sit on the couch. "Wait here, I'll be back in a minute." And with that, she left.

Mina once again took flight in the night sky and hunted as she always did. She found her target and killed it, but this time she brought the body back to the farmhouse.

"Here," she said as she dragged the body to Sam on the couch, "Drink up. Your wounds will heal faster and you won't feel lethargic."

"What about you? You fought, too."

"Eh, I'm fine. That was nothing more than a light workout."

Sam lowered his fangs to the human's neck and fed as Mina taught him to do. When he was done, Mina grabbed his arm and pulled him up off the couch, leading him to their bedroom upstairs. Stripping away their clothing, she watched as Sam got under the blankets and let his head rest against the pillow.

"Are you not joining me?" he asked.

"Not yet. I'm going to take a hot bath first."

"Okay. Well, don't be too long."

Mina turned away and walked to the bathroom where she took her long, and much needed, bath. As the water cooled she grabbed a towel to wrap herself up in, but didn't immediately return to the bedroom. She walked down the stairs and into the living room. She sat on the couch, ignoring the fact she was still wet from her bath. Alone with her thoughts, she could begin to process everything that just went down.

She remembered back to the first time she had killed for another, rather than to simply feed herself. It was late 16th century France and she had only been there for a month. Her thoughts took her through the whole event as if it was yesterday.

It was a rainy day, and the streets were filled with people who were coming home from work or going out for

dinner. Mina sat by the large window of her Paris
apartment and watched as the people below passed by. She
had just recently become a widow, so to conform to societal
standards she was dressed in all black and refrained from
attending any social gatherings that occurred. One full
year of nothing but a lonely and colorless life.

*   'Oh darn', Mina thought to herself with a brief smile.*
She never minded the absence of another- it allowed her to
be more free and open with who she was. She had her
butler, Robert, but otherwise no one came around.

*   A few days had passed by and Mina decided to take a*
short walk since the day had been dreary and cloudy. She
always walked with a black lace umbrella for coverage,
mainly for fashion.

*   As she walked along the sidewalk, she passed by a*
park where some young boys played with a ball. A mile or
so away, she could hear an argument between a father and
his son. The argument may have made Mina aware of the
pair, but the loud smack that occurred brought her full
attention.

*   Mina never stood for an adult to beat a child. She*
began to walk in the direction of the noise and found a
father scolding his son, but not with his voice. The father
was holding a long carriage whip and whipping the boy's
back. Anger overtook Mina and she took action.

"Excuse me!" she called after the father as she hurried to confront him.

"What do you want? I'm busy here," the man replied.

"I can see that, but there are ways to discipline a child, other than tearing into the flesh."

"You will not tell me how to treat my child, unless you want to be next!"

The man cast the whip towards Mina as a warning, but this was, of course, a poor choice.

Mina grabbed the whip with her glove-covered hand and pulled it towards her. The man stood stunned by the action and was absolutely speechless.

"Now, boy, tell me, how often does your father do this to you?"

The boy was hesitant in answering, but said "Everyday ma'am."

"Ah, interesting. Would you mind fetching me something to drink? My walk has made me very thirsty."

The boy ran off and Mina's gaze went back to the father.

"Well, this just won't do."

As soon as the boy was out of sight, Mina grabbed the man by the collar and swiftly dragged him around the corner and pinned him up against a brick wall. His eyes filled with fear and curiosity as he witnessed Mina lift him with no effort.

"Wh-What are you?"

"Your demise," she answered.

She allowed her fangs to drop in front of him, his face becoming pale with horror. Mina lowered the man and wasted no time in biting his neck. Each pull drawing in more and more blood. The man eventually became limp, and just to cover her tracks, she had found a piece of glass laying on the ground beside him. She took it and ran it into his neck where the two small puncture holes were.

After she pulled herself together and verified that there was no blood upon herself, she walked back to the house where the boy was standing with a glass of water.

"Where is my father?" the boy asked.

"He had an errand to run," Mina said as she accepted the glass from him and drank.

"I heard something. It sounded like my father."

"I wouldn't give it any more thought. Just know that your father will no longer be here to place another hand upon you."

Mina began thinking that the boy would probably be upset and go find another adult for help. Instead he threw his arms around her and was grateful for what she had done.

"Thank you, madam."

Mina pulled the boy away from her and gave him a decent smile before she took her leave. For the first time in her life, she felt appreciated.

Mina came back to her reality and realized she had been lost in her thoughts long enough that she could see the sun beginning to rise. The sky began to turn all those wonderful, bright, inspirational colors and she knew she had probably better get back upstairs before Sam started asking questions.

Twenty Four

Transylvania - present day

"Has anyone heard from Dragos? To know if he made it to his destination yet?" Gregor asked his fellow council members.

"I have not, but I assume if anything had happened along his journey, the plane people would have let us know," said Vasile logically.

The men were sitting down for their breakfast and immediately began discussing what they would do when the princess was brought back to them.

"We should provide her with the dress that she wore at her ball before she was sent away," Gregor suggested.

Vasile spoke up, "There is a very good chance she would no longer be able to wear it. Who knows what the princess looks like now."

"We shall gather her subjects and have them waiting for her arrival then," Gregor counter suggested.

"We do not have enough space here to hold that amount of people," Vasile stated.

The two men continued to bounce ideas off one another before the third member had decided to join them.

"We don't have the time for all that. She must be crowned as queen and forced to begin working on her reign. As well as producing an heir," spoke up Radu.

The others nodded in agreement and continued on with their meal. As they finished, Gregor spoke to Radu with confusion in his voice, "Radu, how can the princess produce an heir? There are no other born vampires in existence."

"There is one. But even still, the male does not need to be of vampiric birth."

"When did this become true?"

"T'is always been true. It just has not been known thus due to royal status," Radu continued with the biology lesson, "The matter was never prominent in discussion due to royals always being matched with another of vampiric birth, to keep the line clean. But there were always stories and documents stating that many lines have been crossed due to a clean blood line being dirtied with that of a turned vampire."

The men looked at each other with worry in their eyes and hastily began searching for the phone. Gregor reached the phone first and attempted to call Dragos, to inform him that he must find the princess much quicker than expected. He either must plant his seed in her to create a pure heir, or else they risk the princess dirtying the line with a turned male.

"No answer. I do believe the massive fool did not charge the device," stated Gregor as he ended the call.

"Did anyone think to tell him this information?" Radu asked.

Gregor took his seat and said, "We must hope that the princess has not found a mate and does not become with child before Dragos finds her."

The three of them looked at each other and wondered if a forced pregnancy was necessary, but none of them spoke about it any further.

Radu was the one who excused himself first and made his way back to his bedchamber. Of the three men, Radu was the one who had the most heart and really thought of others feelings while making decisions. He never strayed from the law or an order if his kings demanded, but deep within himself always questioned the morality of it.

Something wasn't sitting right with him as he thought of the princess really not having any say in the matter of her life. The king is gone, so do the laws still apply to her?

What's to say she doesn't take the throne and change everything anyway? What would happen to the council if she chose to get rid of them?

The questions ran through his mind as he sat in his bed chamber alone. "Perhaps it would do the vampire race some good if the princess made some changes" he spoke out to himself.

Downstairs Gregor and Vasile sat in silence as they continued combing through old scrolls and looked for laws pertaining to the princess coming home. They had to make sure everything was in order before they sent word out that the monarchy was established once again.

"This is interesting," said Vasile

Gregor looked up from the scroll he was currently reading through and asked, "What did you find?"

"In order for Wilhelmina to take the throne, she must find a male to mate with. It says here, 'Not one soul shall take the throne themselves. There must be two souls together through marriage.'"

Gregor looked curiously at Vasile, trying to think of who could be the male worthy enough to rule beside the princess.

"There is no other royal besides the princess. Hence the urge for her to produce an heir. Which the law continues, 'No child produced out of wedlock is eligible to rule.'"

"Then how in the world do we complete our task?" Gregor questioned.

"It is my understanding that no law found means no law to enforce."

Gregor agreed with a nod and Vasile took the law to the fireplace and lit the aged parchment on fire. Throwing it into the pit of ash, Gregor joined him and the pair watched as it burned.

"I'm going to leave for the day. Is there anything else you need?" came a female voice from behind them. Their maid stood at the entrance of the dining room and waited for the green light to leave.

"Just one more thing, do you mind helping us with the fireplace? We are having difficulty," said Gregor.

"Well, I'm not very good, either, but I can try."

The maid walked over to the fireplace and ignored the burning paper. She did what was needed to get things rolling and just like that, the fire was started.

"Thank you my dear. Now you are dismissed," Vasile stated with gratitude.

She made her exit and, once the front door was closed behind her, Gregor and Vasile shared a look of secrecy then moved back to the table where they continued their work.

Twenty Five

Sam was the first to wake up and he was happy to see that Mina was still in his arms fast asleep. He kissed her neck and removed himself from behind her to get out of bed. He walked to the bathroom to take care of business, then walked past their bedroom and down the stairs.

Looking at the clock on the wall, it was 8pm and he really wanted to go check on everyone at the camp now that his father was no longer alive.

Figuring Mina wouldn't mind him doing a welfare check on his friends, Sam slipped on his boots and jogged over to the camp. When he arrived, he was horrified at what he saw. Tents were destroyed, personal belongings were strewn about, and bodies had been left out to be claimed by the sun. The few people who were left smiled when they saw Sam.

"Sam!" called a woman. Sam knew her as Mary.

"Hey, are you okay? What happened here?" Sam inquired with genuine concern.

"Your father changed somehow and took out anyone in his path. Everyone is dead except for a handful of us."

Sam was both angered and saddened by his father's choices and the results of them.

"I'm so sorry he did this, but I can assure you he won't be coming around anymore."

"Why? He said he would be back to finish the job."

"I promise, he won't. He… can't."

As she figured out what he was trying to say, she took a sigh of relief and left it at that. Sam continued on with his check of the camp and those who remained. Another person came up to him, "Sam, what do we do? Where do we go?"

"I'm not your boss. You can do whatever you like."

"But, how did you and your father become so… strong?"

Sam thought long about what his answer should be. After a long pause he said, "Do you want to be a vampire? Do you want to continue to live with no death in your future? If so, then you have to feed on a human. Don't be greedy but the blood of a human will take care of you. If you'd rather stay as you are or be done with it, don't do anything and go find a life for yourself. It's your choice now."

He walked away after his statement. He didn't want the responsibility of being the decision maker for others.

Sam came to his father's tent and looked around. There was a path that went from one side of the tent to the other. "So, he planned it all out," Sam said to himself.

He started to turn away when he spotted a trunk on the side that was locked. Sam walked over to it and broke the lock off with ease. Inside contained memories of the human life Sam and his father left behind. Pictures, documents, baby clothes and...

Sam paused when he saw the small box on top of some old baby photos. He opened it up and it revealed 2 silver wedding bands. It was his father and mothers set when they were married. Unfortunately, his mother died when he was born, and he feels like that's when his father began to decline mentally. Closing the ring box, he set it back in its place and closed the trunk as well.

As Sam stood up, his phone went off. A text from Mina made him smile as he read the screen, 'Where are you? I'm ready to go get something to eat.' He replied to her text and then shoved the phone back into the pocket of his jeans.

Sam went over to his tent and gathered what little clothes he still had, although nothing really fit him anymore. 'Guess I need to go shopping,' he thought to himself.

Sam left the clothes, grabbed the trunk and headed home. He couldn't help but notice Jessica was missing from the welcome committee. That's when he saw the burned grass by the garden. She always spent her time there, and she must have been his first victim. Sam wasn't necessarily saddened by this, but she wasn't a bad person either to deserve such a death.

Sam continued walking the opposite direction of the garden and made his way out to the field.

****

Mina woke up to an empty bed, and an empty house for that matter.

Confused, she looked at her phone and saw the time. She assumed then that Sam went to check on the people at the camp. She sent him a quick text and left it at that. God, she was starving.

Mina got out of bed and made her way downstairs and made herself some coffee. She felt her phone vibrate and saw Sam's reply, which made her smile. Placing her phone down on the counter, she made her coffee and, as always, drank it black.

She decided to take advantage of the night and go sit on her back porch. The moon was high in the sky and it illuminated the entire field. She gazed up at the stars and for once, she was genuinely happy. Looking out into the wide open space before her, she saw a figure walking towards her. 'Sam' she said in her mind.

Only wearing a t-shirt and panties, she ran off to meet him. She was bounding over to him when she saw him carrying something.

"What's that?"

"Memories, and um, excuse me for this but, WHY THE FUCK ARE YOU OUT HERE WITH NO PANTS ON?"

Mina paid him no attention and chuckled, "Memories, huh? Nice. I'd love to see them."

Sam stood there in the wide open and just stared at her, speechless.

"Sam, no one is out here to see me. Get over it."

"The birds, deer, bears...."

"Lions and tigers too?" she said to him mockingly.

"Get your ass back inside. Now."

"Or what? What are you gonna do about it?"

Before Sam could react, he watched as his female removed more clothing and then began to jog back to the house. Sam was turned on and frustrated at the same time. He caught up with her, dropped the trunk, and scooped her up into his arms.

"No one. And I mean no one, is allowed to see you like this except for me."

"And what happens if someone does?" she said back flirtatiously, really pushing his buttons.

"They die." He said with a serious face. Mina brushed the side of his face with her hand and said, "Aw, you're cute when you get possessive."

As Sam carried her into the farmhouse he couldn't help but roll his eyes at her. They continued laughing with each other as they reached the porch and Sam lowered her down. Yet he didn't move away from her until she was in the house, where no prying eyes could have the chance to see her.

Mina walked into the house and stood there at the door, waiting for Sam to come back after he picked up the trunk. Once inside, Sam lowered the hefty item to the ground and went back to his female. Grabbing her by her waist and pulling her in close, he said, "We need to talk".

Mina pulled away from him and looked into those ocean blue eyes of his. He was serious and had a hint of sadness in his voice.

"Something happened at the camp, didn't it?"

Sam pulled his shirt off and gave it to Mina so she could be clothed while he told her what he saw. She took the shirt and got into serious mode as they walked to the couch. While she gave him her undivided attention, he told her everything. Mina was saddened for Sam, but not surprised, given the power trip his father had been on.

"Sam, I'm so sorry. Those people didn't deserve that. But, what happens to the ones who survived?" Mina asked.

"I told them I'm not a leader, and that they have a few options, but they must decide for themselves." He continued, "I won't be responsible for those people. They have their own lives to live and they are more than capable of handling themselves."

"Sam, I get what you're saying, but they don't know how to hunt. They may need a little guidance."

"I'm not helping them. I suppose if someone were to knock on the door and ask, then maybe. But I'm not going back to the camp."

With that, Mina stood up and said, "I need to feed. I'm starving and I figure you could use something as well."

Sam was looking at her as the meal she was, only wearing his shirt. MIna immediately picked up on what he was thinking, "No sir, maybe later, but I mean a real meal."

Sam sat back on the couch like a child being told no, but quickly recovered as he, too, rose from the couch and looked down to her. "Okay, let's go out. Then after, I'll do what I want to you."

Giggling like love struck teenagers, Mina and Sam ran up the stairs to get dressed. Well, mainly Mina, since Sam already had clothes on.

"Hey, can we swing by a store? I need new clothes since…"

"We can order them online. Nothing is open right now, but I'm sure they will be here by tomorrow." Mina began to talk to herself in her head, 'Goodness, if only Amazon Prime existed back then, people wouldn't have to go out and search for something. What a luxury." Surprisingly, Mina did have a debit card, but her bank was under a different name, so no one could track her.

Before heading out, Mina opened Amazon on her phone and let Sam pick out some things. About $300 later, Sam's wardrobe was selected and would be there tomorrow afternoon.

They left the house on a mission for dinner. They knew what- or rather who- they would be having for dessert. Mina took the lead, with Sam close behind her. Mina was happy and she felt as though nothing could ruin things for her now.

Little did she know what was awaiting her in the days to come.

Twenty Six

Dragos reached the place called Savannah, Georgia, five days after he landed in Atlanta. He could feel the hairs on his arms rise and a flowery scent in the air. "Princess," he said to himself.

He began searching as he sensed she was close. There were people out that night, drinking and dancing, sometimes gawking at him due to his sheer size and looks. Dragos was attractive but scary as well. He could lure a female in with his looks, but easily destroy her due to his inability to care for others.

Dragos walked around and when he turned a corner that led to a new street, across the way, there she was. She looked exactly as she did when he had last seen her. Long flowy black hair and an unforgiving face of beauty. Dragos was hesitant to approach her due to not having a true plan to take her.

That's when a tall male came up behind her and grabbed her waist. Seeing her laugh showed him that this male was hers. Competition was always something Dragos enjoyed. A good challenge just to show that he was the better male of the race.

He observed the pair walking along the semi-empty street. Sticking to the shadows, Dragos followed them, but not too close, for he knew the princess would sense his presence. He observed them hunt, laugh, and also get some human food. The night was seemingly over, due to the way they spoke and how they began walking towards the city's exit.

Like a predator stalking its prey, he stayed on their tail. He stopped on a dime as the princess turned towards where he had been walking.

"What's wrong?" the tall black haired male asked her.

"It feels like we are being followed. But I'm not sure who. It feels... familiar," the princess replied to the male.

Taking the princess by the hand, he pulled her in his direction to keep walking, "Well, come on. You still owe me that dessert you promised me," he told her.

The princess replied to him with a giggle, "Oh you are bad."

"I collect my debts."

Dragos stayed put for a while before continuing on. He watched how they interacted with each other and it made him sick. He never cared for love or anything close to it. Sex was for fun, dominance, or procreating. That's it. And, he had no problem using his shaft to show a female who's boss.

The walk continued for another ten miles and finally the disgustingly happy pair made it to a small white house that was slightly set back from the road. He could hear everything the two of them were getting into. As soon as they entered the house, he heard the moans and the heavy breathing as their bodies came together.

Without taking anymore of this behavior, Dragos walked to the wooded area off the right side of the house and made sure he found a spot that was close but didn't have her scent. Just so he knew that she wouldn't be walking in his direction.

The planning was a task. He had to figure out how to trap the princess and how to get her to come back to Romania. He knew that being a member of the royal family made her severely stronger than most, but he could outsmart her. He wouldn't rush the process, but he knew there was some kind of deadline before the council was after him about his duty.

****

Five days later......

Mina woke to her phone ringing. She looked at the screen and didn't recognise the number. "Damn telemarketers," she said as she rolled back over to find Sam, laying there still asleep. 'How lucky am I?' she thought to herself as she admired what was hers.

While she admired her male, she decided it was as good a time as any to just start the day. She walked over to the window in the upstairs landing across from her bedroom, and saw that it was raining. A soothing, steady rain was hitting the farmhouse roof in a rhythm that could put anyone to sleep.

Mina always liked the rain. It calmed her. With it being November though, things were getting a little chilly for her liking. She walked back into her room and found a pair of black baggy sweatpants and a dark blue crew neck sweatshirt and slipped both on.

She made her way down the stairs and when she reached the first floor, she noticed something was off. A feeling she could not quite identify made her feel uneasy. She walked over to the backdoor and looked out its window. Seeing nothing out of the ordinary, she went out to the porch. No wind, just rain coming down as if the sky sprung a massive leak.

Looking around she saw nothing, but was shocked when two large arms came from behind and wrapped around her.

"Asshole!" Mina shouted out as Sam came from behind to grab her.

"Me? No way. I just wanted to come see what you were doing."

She looked him over and of course he was still in his black basketball shorts and no shirt. Male vampires typically ran a hotter temperature than humans. Even in the middle of winter they could be out there with no clothes and be comfortable.

Feeling flirty, she noticed that he didn't have any boxers on, so she took her right hand and trailed it down his chest, stomach, and then to the top of his shorts. When she reached the top of the band, she slid her hand down inside and found what she was wanting. She heard the growl in Sam's chest as she grabbed him and began teasing the head. While doing this she was backing him into the house and asking, "Want some coffee?" she removed her hand and went into the kitchen.

"Okay, now who is the asshole?" he asked as he glanced down at the hard protrusion in his shorts.

"Eh, it's payback. Now, coffee?"

Mina made them a pot and they sat on the couch while they watched the rain together.

"Sam, I have a question."

"Yes?"

"How do you feel about kids?"

The question popped up out of nowhere and Sam looked at her in surprise. She sat up and looked at him.

With hesitation Sam replied, "Kids? Well, when I was human I knew I always wanted to be a father. I never really found anyone who I liked enough to have a kid with. I was turned before I could find 'the one', so I gave up on the idea," he answered.

"Ah, okay," was all she said back to him.

"Mina, what's on your mind? What are you thinking about?"

"Well, I never gave kids much thought because when I was a kid myself, I never thought I'd be a good mom and then I met Dimitri and things changed. But, we know how that ended and I never wanted anyone close to me like that. Until you."

"Mina", Sam began with a question, "Can vampires reproduce?"

Mina looked at him and answered, "Well, in all honesty, I know that born vampires can. I heard stories about some being born of both lines. I do think that two who are both turned, though, can't procreate."

She saw Sam begin deep into his thoughts, "Sam?"

He looked up to her and she continued hesitantly, "When I was young, no one informed me of how a child was even created. What I know I've learned through the years as I traveled. I can't answer your questions with facts. Only assumptions."

Mina got up, walked over to the sink and placed her now empty mug into it. She looked up and out the kitchen window into the woods in front of her. Her instincts told her that someone was out there. That someone was watching her, but she didn't know who.

"Sam?"

"Yeah?" Sam said, still sitting in the living room.

"I'll be right back, will you stay here?"

As soon as the words left her mouth, Sam was at her side.

"Why? What's wrong?"

She always admired the way he was so protective over her. She never had that from a male, not even her father.

"Nothing, I think I just want to go for a walk."

"I'm not comfortable with you going out alone."

"Sam, my dear Sam. I love that you want to be my protector, and I'll let you. But remember, I can take care of myself." Mina saw the sadness in his eyes as she spoke, but Sam quickly agreed and asked that she come back in an hour so he didn't worry.

She grabbed a rain jacket she found in the coat closet down stairs and slid on her tennis shoes. Sam was waiting for her by the backdoor and she gave him a long kiss. "I love you," she said as she left. She had never said that to anyone, not even her first love. Not out loud anyway. After she made her claim, she began to walk away but was stopped short when Sam grabbed her by her bicep and pulled her back to him.

Giving her a long, solid kiss, he cupped her face with both his hands and said, "I love you, too."

Mina smiled the most genuine of smiles at him and left out the door and down the steps. She went to the side of the house and vanished into the woods.

Twenty Seven

Watching his female leave him was the most difficult and frustrating thing Sam had encountered so far. He knew she wanted some time to herself, but hated he couldn't be there with her. Of course, he knew that she could take on five times what he could, but it was just the point. Sam used his hearing to seek out Mina to make sure she was still walking and breathing. Unfortunately his range wasn't the best so he heard the sound of her fade and then she was too far out.

Sam figured that since he was alone he would do some housekeeping around the place to pass the time. He loaded the washer and emptied the dryer, folded clothes and put them away. He moved up to their room and tidied it up then made his way to the bathroom.

He got the cleaning products out and began scrubbing the tub, sink, floor and even washed the window. He put the cleaning supplies back into the supply closet where they kept the towels and continued his work to the kitchen. After all was said and done, he looked at his phone. His face dropped when he realized it had only been 30 minutes.

So, he did what any respectable man would do. He walked his sad ass to the back porch and sat down on the floor with his back against the house. He was like a lost puppy waiting for its owner to come home. But, Mina was worth the wait, and he was so thankful he found someone he could be happy with.

Sam sat there for so long, he couldn't feel his cheeks underneath him. Pulling out his phone once more, he saw that Mina had 3 minutes to get home before he told her that he would start to worry. 3 minutes, 2 minutes, 1 minute...... time. Sam used his hearing to listen for her but heard nothing.

He stood up and shook his ass a little to get the blood pumping again, and walked back into the house. He jogged down the basement steps and grabbed a fresh pair of black sweatpants from the dryer and some tall socks. Once he got back to the first floor, he put his black boots on and hit the trail running. Every five feet or so he would stop and try to sense her. Still nothing. "Where the fuck could she be?" he asked himself. Panic was beginning to rise in his chest and mind as he was plenty far from the house and still had no sign of her.

Sam felt he walked and ran all over the property and still had no sign of her. No sign of anyone else- even the camp was now empty.

He tried her cell, but then remembered that she left it in the house before leaving.

Sam let out a ferocious male howl as he let out his frustration,

"Dammit!". It had been four hours now and she wasn't anywhere close.

"Come on baby, where are you?" He spoke to the air with no one to listen. He decided to head back to the house to see if maybe she was there. He couldn't hear her, but maybe she was just being quiet. As he came up to the porch, things were as he left them. No change, no sign that another had come in.

Sam sat on the porch in the rain and pondered what his next move should be.

****

Dragos was nearly finished with his plan. He had to finalize some of the details, but otherwise he was ready. And almost as if on cue, he heard someone walking in the woods where he was residing. He smelled the air and to his surprise, it was her. The princess had foolishly come right to him. But she was walking parallel to where he was and he had made sure to use animal scent to mask his own. He knew well how to survive in the wilderness and made sure to cover all his bases. He continued to watch the princess while she walked and he tracked her every move.

'Why are you alone my princess?' he wondered mentally. He began to walk but made sure of every step he took, so he did not make noise and get her to see him. He was far enough away from the house, but not far enough to where he couldn't sense them either.

He questioned why she was continuing to go further and further from the house. He reminded himself that Mina was smart, but he needed to be smarter. He listened for her male, not that he cared about the bastard, but heard nothing.

He was right on her heels, but then the princess dropped to her knees.

Confused, Dragos placed himself behind a tree and slowed his heart so she couldn't pick up on it. And then he smelled it, the salt from tears. 'Crying?' he wondered, 'Why would the princess be crying?'

Then he heard her, "Mother, if you are out there, or can hear me in heaven. Please help me now. I love him, and I never thought I would find love after Dimitri. And I want to bear his children, but know not of the process before and after conception. I am lost mother and I need guidance."

'Want children?' Dragos questioned in his head, 'Children with that turned bastard who would dirty the royal line?' Dragos kept his temperament at bay so as to not alarm the princess that she was not alone. He kept listening as she pleaded with the dead.

"Mother, why didn't you teach me these things? Please, help me from the grave and show me what I can expect if my dreams were to come true."

He watched as she stayed on her knees, crying. She certainly was a lost little lamb, and the big bad wolf was here to take her away.

From the far distance, he could hear a male cry out of anger. It was her male, the turned fool who she wanted to continue her line with. He saw Mina rise to her feet with haste and run as quickly as she could back in the direction she came from.

"Too distracted to notice her surroundings," he said after she ran right past him. "So infatuated with him, she willingly lets her guard down, too," he continued. Dragos walked back towards his 'camp' and sat as he ironed out his details and slightly modified his plan. 'This may be easier than expected,' he commented internally.

Twenty Eight

After Mina said her prayer to her mother in the afterlife, she realized she did not know how far she had walked or how long she had been gone for. She patted herself and realized she also didn't think to get her phone. That's when she heard the primal shout coming from the direction of the house.

'Sam,' she thought.

She rose to her feet immediately and began to run as fast as she could. She passed by a specific tree that felt like someone was there, but didn't smell like anything other than an animal. She continued on to home and was shocked when she broke through the tree line.

Sam was sitting on the steps in the pouring rain, no shirt, and his body was steaming from his internal heat. He looked at her with eyes so dark, she could tell he was upset because she didn't return in the time frame he requested.

Within a split second, he rushed over and scooped her up and planted a hard kiss on her. Then he whispered in her ear, "You're late." Out in the wide open, he picked her up and pushed her against the closest tree. One hand held her in place while the other ripped her pants from her body.

She was on full display where anyone passing by could see them but she saw that he didn't care. "I need you." Sam said to her with a hungry growl in his tone. "Then have me," Mina said as she used her hands to free what was necessary for them to be joined at the hips.

Sam wasted no time in slamming himself into her, over and over. Mina gasped as he repeatedly entered her and pulled out. The thrusting of his hips was so intense that Mina came right away. Sam came shortly after her and both were panting in each other's ear as Sam rested his head on her shoulder, still connected to one another. His length retreated from her on its own and Sam gently lowered his female back on her feet.

"Are you okay? I'm not mad, but what was that about?" Mina asked as Sam helped her with her pants before his own.

"I thought something had happened to you, and when you reappeared, something inside of me took over and all I knew was that I had to be inside you."

Mina looked at him with sincerity in her eyes, "I'm sorry, my love. I was in my head and didn't realize how far out I had gone. I had something to work through mentally and when I was done, I heard you yell."

"You heard that?"

"Yes, I did. And when I did, I came back here as quickly as I could. Next time, I'll take my phone with me."

Sam laughed, "Next time? Nope, we are never separating again."

The pair of them walked off towards the house and Mina glanced back over her shoulder as if she sensed something, but brushed it off as an animal. And there was definitely an animal watching them, only he walked on two legs instead of four.

Once they reached the inside, Sam said, "How about a hot bath to get rid of the chill?" Mina knew well enough that Sam didn't have a chill and neither did she really. It sounded nice, but she really wasn't in the mood, "That's okay, maybe later."

Sam looked over at her from the hallway as she stayed by the backdoor as if waiting for something.

"What is it?"

"It's nothing," Mina replied.

"It's not nothing. I can tell something is wrong."

"It's just…", Mina's thoughts trailed off as she looked around the house. "Did you clean?" she asked.

"I did. I needed something to distract me while you were gone. But, it didn't distract me for long."

Mina was taken by a male cleaning, well, anything. From what she grew up with and what she had witnessed through the years, the women or females did that kind of work.

"It looks great in here, thank you," she said with admiration.

Well, I live here now so I figured I can help out."

Mina thought for a second about how things were moving quite quickly. She didn't mind it as it was not a bad thing, it was just a fact. They had only known each other for about six months and they were already living together.

"You good?" said Sam as he sounded concerned why she was staring at him with a blank look on her face.

"Yeah, sorry, just in my thoughts."

"So what happened out there?"

"Nothing, I just had to talk to someone. My mother." Mina gave him the details of her adventure and he stood there focused on her words. As she finished up, she said, "Sometimes I wish I had my mother's guidance. Or, really any guidance on how the vampire female body works. It's somewhat embarrassing that I'm 500 plus years old and don't know much about myself in that way." Mina lowered her head in shame but her chin was lifted by two large fingers, which directed her face to look at her male.

"There is nothing to be ashamed of. I know things back then were different for women, uh, females."

The look in her eyes held so much appreciation, she didn't have to say a word.

"I'm going to lay down for a while. I'm just tired all of a sudden," Mina said as she pulled herself away from Sam.

"Alright, I'm going to stay down here and read a book I found while cleaning."

They shared a kiss and parted ways. Mina walked up the stairs and as soon as she reached her bed, she was out like a light.

****

Mina opened her eyes and realized she was back in Transylvania. 'I must be dreaming', she thought to herself in her dream.

"Mina, you must hurry. Father and mother are waiting on us to join them for breakfast," came an all too familiar voice.

"Ana?" Mina looked in the direction of the voice and there she was. Her dear sister, whom she lost all those years ago.

"Come on, we must go down now," Ana said with impatience in her voice. Mina realised she was already dressed for the day and her hair had been placed high off her shoulders. Moving quickly she followed her second

eldest sister through the castle, down multiple hallways and into the wide open room they ate meals in.

There, at the long wooden table by the grand fireplace, was her family. Father at the head, mother beside him, Natahlia already discussing matters pertaining to the ball and Ana taking her seat next to Natahlia. Mina couldn't help but feel tears straining to break free of her eyes and she observed her family, the one she hadn't seen in over 500 years.

"Mina, my dear, come sit and eat. You must have something before today's festivities begin," came the sweet sound of her mothers voice.

Obeying her mother, the queen, Mina walked quickly to the seat next to her and just stared. Mina was amazed at how real the dream was. She thought for a moment that perhaps she had died after she fell asleep.

"Wilhelmina, eat. Do as you're told, girl." The booming sound was from her father. He was a large male that was most feared and with good reason. Mina was rebellious, but not to the extent of angering her father.

"Yes, father," Mina said as she looked at her plate. Yet, there was nothing to be eaten. Her plate was clean of any food that had been prepared, which her family was enjoying immensely.

"Right, today is a big day. You all have duties tonight, not just to dance with eligible male suitors but to mingle with others as well," stated her father.

"Yes father," her two sisters said in unison. Mina remained silent. 'The ball?' she questioned mentally. Mina was silent and frozen after she realized that she was back at the day where she would watch Dimitri die. With urgency, Mina rose from her spot at the table and ran off without any word. She didn't make it far when she nearly ran into a sort of wall. Looking up she saw him, "Dragos," she said.

"Princess, please return to your seat and finish your meal. I am required, as well as your maid, to keep you from leaving the castle and to keep you on schedule."

Mina never cared much for following orders, but she also knew she wanted to spend whatever time she had in this dream, with her family.

Reluctantly she went back to her seat and just listened to the conversation that was being had. Her sisters were discussing matters of certain lords they were looking forward to dancing with, mother was giving advice for them not to seem too eager and her father was reading over laws that the council had written.

"Mother, may I speak with you?" Mina asked.

As if in some sort of strange film, her mother looked at her and took her hand.

"Wilhelmina my dear, I know. I heard you."

As if someone blew out the candles from the massive chandelier that hung from the great high ceiling, the room went dark.

****

Mina woke from her dream confused more than anything. 'She heard me?' Mina questioned. Mina sat up and she was back in her room at the farmhouse. That had to have been the most realistic dream, so much that she still felt her mothers touch upon her hand. Mina almost began to cry, but held back her tears so Sam wouldn't sense them. She wanted to be alone for a little while, to just take it in and really process what she had just encountered. She decided to check the time and her phone revealed that three hours had passed by. Looking out the window, she saw it was still raining and according to the weather app on her phone, it was going to rain for a couple more days. Continuing to look out the window, she softly said, "Oh, mother, how I miss you so."

Twenty Nine

Dragos was patiently waiting for his opportune moment to capture the princess. Not that he felt anyone was a true threat, but because he didn't want to take a chance on not succeeding. He was waiting behind the tree line and didn't see or hear any movement from within the house.

A couple days had passed since the princess walked right by him and didn't even realise she was being watched. His plan of wearing animal blood and deer pelt had worked well to hide his scent and identity.

As the night enveloped the sky and the land became dark, Dragos prepared to make his move. He began hearing movement in the house and realized that Sam, the male, was the first to awaken. He could hear Sam walking down the steps to the first floor and watched as the kitchen light came on. Dragos walked out into the open field, where he knew he would be seen by the male. He wanted to fight. He knew he would beat this male and could use him as leverage against the princess.

"Alright, let's do this," Dragos said out loud to himself. He took his first steps forward, staring at the male, waiting to be seen.

****

Ever since the other day, Mina had not had any dreams like the one where she was with her family. She spent the last twenty four hours relaxing with Sam and talking to him about her dream. Things were simple and she enjoyed being able to relax with no worries, no threats.

When Mina awoke, she heard a loud thud come from downstairs. 'What is he doing down there?' she thought. Mina got out of bed and threw on some black sweatpants and a t-shirt, and made her way down the stairs.

"Sam?" she called out into the seemingly empty house. She quickly walked around and found no sign of her male. The panic began to set in, as she knew there was nowhere else Sam would have wandered off to.

She opened her senses and began tracking him. She could smell him, so he had in fact been downstairs at some point, but was no longer in the house. She made her way to the back porch and that's when she saw him.

"No, it can't be," she protested.

"Hello, your highness," Dragos said.

'Shit' she cursed mentally. How had he survived the attack? Where had he been all these years? The questions began running through her mind. But one thing was for sure. He had Sam and she would be damned if she let another male die because of her. Especially one she loved.

"What do you want?" she asked.

"You. You need to come with me at the council's request."

"I'm not taking the throne, Dragos. The monarchy died with my family."

"You wanna bet?"

He picked Sam up by his neck and bit him. There was no benefit to either male when one bit another, but it was a sign of dominance. Oh, that pissed her off. The energy shooting off her was enough to blow the light bulbs in the house. She immediately released her dark side and leapt from the porch, getting between Sam and Dragos before anything else could be done.

Before she could reach her male, Dragos tossed Sam to the side like a sack of potatoes and got into a fighting stance himself. Mina knew she was dealing with a vampire who was even older than her, but Mina had been working on her fighting skills since he last saw her.

The two collided and the wrestling match began. Each took turns being on top and dealing out punches, then the other would gain control and apply the same. Mina finally had him pinned down to the ground and he seemingly wasn't going anywhere.

She looked over at Sam to check and make sure he was okay. It's no fault of his own that he was no match for Dragos since Sam could never have prepared for such a fight. But, without even thinking about it, she had just broken her top rule in combat. She broke her eye contact from the threat, and as she was distracted. She gave her opponent the perfect opportunity to gain leverage. With one swift motion, Dragos was able to break free from her and now he was the one on top.

There was a sharp pain at her side, and then another in her back. The pain was there, but nothing she hadn't felt before, it was still manageable. Without even noticing, she realized that there was a rope around her neck, which was becoming tighter and tighter. That was when she lost her vision and time became insignificant.

About twenty minutes later, Mina began to open her eyes and the world was brought back to her. She still had the rope at her neck, but now, she was bound in other places. Her wrists, her knees, and her ankles, all had their own prison.

Mina looked around and no longer saw Sam. That was when she became desperate for answers. Throwing herself around like a fish out of water, Mina made every effort to

escape what bound her. Yet, she had no luck. The rope was
so tight on her, that even her own strength was no match.

Out of nowhere, she heard heavy footsteps
approaching, it was Dragos.

"Where is he?" she demanded.

"Don't worry, he has a good seat to the show."

"Show? What show? As a servant to the crown, you
have no power to do this."

"On the contrary, my princess, I was told to bring you
back with whatever means necessary."

"I'll kill you no matter what, but I'll make it quick if
you let him go."

"Oh, no, you won't have that opportunity."

"Oh? And why is that?"

"Because you are going back to where you belong and
he is staying here. Bound. In front of a window where he
can see everything happening right now. Don't worry, he
still has one eye he can see out of."

Mina's eyes opened wide and she knew she needed to
get to Sam. Making one last attempt to get free, Mina was
able to shift her arms enough away from each other so she
could free her wings. They broke free from her and she
attempted to use them to hit Dragos. She landed one good
hit, but of course it wouldn't actually take him down.
Dragos regained his footing, stepped forward and grabbed
onto her wings so she could no longer move them.

"Ready for the fun to begin?" Dragos asked her, not expecting an actual reply.

"What? What fu-" Mina was cut off by a type of pain she hadn't felt before. She was on her stomach and couldn't look over her shoulder, but she imagined that he was sliding some sort of knife into the root of her wings. One for each. Mina screamed as he performed this torture on her, and ultimately paralyzed her.

"Won't it be difficult princess? For you to take flight with no wings?" Dragos whispered, "I also believe that the council will find it interesting that you have a hidden gift."

Mina could feel eyes on her as she eventually gave into the pain and accepted that if she stayed still, the pain would disappear.

After a few minutes of silence, Mina said, "Just wait until I am free from these things that bind me, and you will have no life to live."

"Oh, dear princess, threats do not scare me. I do, however, have a question for you." Confused, Mina looked at him the best she could.

Trying to be witty she replied, "Yes. You are a dick. And yes, you are the epitome of a useless male."

Dragos laughed and said, "Princess Mina, do you know what happens to smart mouth females who forget their place and have a male who is supposed to protect them, but cannot?"

"I'm not sure, but I sense you're about to tell me... 'oh wise one'."

Mina knew damn well that she was provoking him. It wasn't like her to take any form of punishment or violence without some form of sarcasm. Dragos moved behind her and Mina watched him over her shoulder and he moved his hands to the tie at his pants.

"They are reminded that the male they are with is inferior," he said.

With that Mina began to move as much as she could, which with being bound, wasn't very far. She didn't quite know what he meant by that but it couldn't be anything good. Next thing she knew, there was a lot of weight at her back, as if she was being pushed further into the ground. She began to feel a slight breeze between her legs, as if her pants had been removed, but remained on at the same time.

"What are you-" Mina cut herself off when she glanced over her shoulder and saw that Dragos had released a large member from his pants and it was ready for action.

"Now princess, hold still."

She struggled as much as she could, just to make it harder on him. She couldn't believe the position she was in right now, both figuratively and literally. She felt him hit her in the back of the head, hard enough to make her lose focus for a moment. But a moment was all he needed. A

second later, she was face down in the dirt and her hips
were lifted up off the ground. Feeling more exposed than
when she ever was with Sam, Mina was no longer in
control.

Mina felt something large enter her from behind and
knew that there was no way out of it. Dragos slammed his
pelvis against her, while his length was sliding in and out.
It seemed like forever but when he finished, she felt herself
become full of him. She felt defeated in a way she had
never felt in her whole existence. He pulled himself away
from her and she could hear him doing up his pants.

There was something else she heard, a whimper.
'Sam', she thought. Sam must have been watching the
whole time. Which of course was Dragos' plan all along.

Dragos lifted Mina up, put her over his shoulder and
took her away. For the first time in her life, she gave up.
She may have been defeated but at least her male was still
alive. At least, that's what she told herself. With the knives
still in her back, every movement made over Drago's
shoulder was unbearable. She decided to close her eyes and
drift off from the pain.

Thirty

Sam sat in that empty house for days after his Mina was taken. He had no energy to fight and felt he couldn't escape the grasp of the cold chains that were wrapped around him and that chair he was in. He was finding it hard to think of anything else other than what happened that night with that male.

He was so much stronger than Sam had expected, no matter how hard he fought for Mina. The images continued to flash through his mind of Mina being under that male, being taken against her will. The fact that Sam couldn't do anything to stop it made him feel weak and that he wasn't the right male to protect her. 'Perhaps the other male won for a reason,' Sam thought.

Sam sat there for what seemed like forever as he decided to give up and waste away. Sam drifted off into his own mental space to pass the time.

"Sam!" came a voice from behind him. Sam turned around quickly trying to catch a body to put with the voice that was calling for him. Yet, no one was there. The voice continued to repeat and was causing Sam to have whiplash from the multiple directions it seemed to be coming from. He couldn't tell if the voice was female or male, and it was unrecognizable.

Finally, Sam turned around once more and there stood a person, someone he didn't know. It was another male. He was about as tall as Sam with dark hair and had on a black robe of some kind.

"Go to her," said the male.

"How? I don't know where she has been taken," Sam replied.

"Go to the place she once called home."

"Once called home? She never told me where home was!" Sam said as his frustration grew.

"Go to her," the voice continued to repeat.

Hearing the voice over and over again threw him into anger. He lunged forward at the robed figure, yet passed right through. Looking behind him, the figure was gone but he could still hear the voice telling him to 'go to her'.

Sam stayed on his knees and covered his ears, and after a brief moment, the voice stopped. Sam looked up and

saw a green field, turning around he also saw a large
castle. He began hearing a voice, a female voice.

"Wilhelmina, you must come in at once! Your father
will be furious if he knows you've been out since dinner. It's
almost dawn!" said a woman standing at the castle base,
just inside a wooden double door.

"I'm coming!" Came a familiar voice, but it sounded
much more innocent.

Sam looked to his left and there in the field was a
female, maybe 12, riding a large black horse. They were
going in circles and the young girl had a huge smile on her
face. A face which he recognised. 'Mina', he said. He had
never seen such joy in her eyes.

All of a sudden many flashbacks occurred, flashbacks
that were not his. It was like a movie playing before him of
multiple scenes from her life, Mina's past. What she told
him of Dimitri, her father, bits of her life through all her
years up till she met him. As the memories moved faster,
they came to an abrupt halt and everything went black.

A small light glowed and the robed male reappeared,
"She needs you, go to her."

Sam stood in shock, still trying to grasp everything he
just saw.

"Who are you?" he asked.

"I'm only a memory" the male replied.

As if all the air from his lungs was sucked out, Sam was pulled away from the male.

Sam opened his eyes and lifted his head. He had never had something like that happen before, no dream was ever as real as that was. But Sam had a new found determination that was exactly what he needed to go after his female.

Sam was still bound in his chains but he allowed his rage to build and he used every muscle in his body to try and break free. Out of frustration, he stood up and threw himself backwards to break the wooden chair he was sitting in. Success.

Sam loosened the chains enough to slip free and stand up, which was easier said than done as he had not been on his feet for a while. As his muscles remembered how to hold him up and his legs became more sturdy, Sam walked to the bedroom that he and Mina had shared. He looked around and decided to change his clothes, then walked down stairs to make himself some coffee while he tried to figure out where he was in the dream.

Thinking he could use his phone to look up some places that may match the picture in his head, he realized he did not know where it was, but then remembered he left it upstairs to charge since it was dead.

He sat at the small table in the kitchen for a while, then began to think about what Mina said about her family line. "Didn't she say her grandfather was Dracula?" Sam asked himself. "Wasn't he always known for being in Transylvania?"

Sam decided that he needed to head overseas, yet he cut that idea off real quick once he realized that he didn't have a passport. A few hours passed and the sun decided to make an appearance, so he definitely was not going outside now. He needed time to plan anyway, so he took advantage of the daytime to make some calls.

Heading back upstairs, Sam grabbed his phone off the charger and began googling information about getting a passport quickly or what would happen if you try to leave the country without a passport. Search after search resulted in Sam finally finding what he was looking for. He made a couple phone calls and submitted a few things online, paid a fee with the untraceable piece of plastic Mina showed him, and he was done.

After what seemed like an eternity, Sam received his emergency passport. He bought himself a plane ticket and went to the bedroom to pack a bag, including only the necessities. Phone charger, wallet, a change of clothes, etc.

Once he was finished, he looked at his phone and saw there was still a few hours until the sun would go down.

Sam thought about what he would do once he reached his destination, what he would do to find Mina. His rescue planning began.

Thirty One

The sound of traffic brought Mina out from her daze as she opened her eyes long enough to see where she was. She didn't recognize anything, so she doubted she was still in the States.

Mina had been in and out of consciousness for a few days now while she was forced to travel with Dragos. Her head was pounding and her back was in so much pain, she forced herself to pass out. She never spoke, she had no strength to fight, and she was starving. It had been so long since she fed that she didn't have much will to do anything except submit to whatever was coming her way.

When conscious, she would try and pass her time thinking of Sam, telling herself that he was alive and well. She wondered if he missed her as much as she missed him, and if he would try to come looking for her. Part of her hoped he would stay put and move on without her so he stayed safe, but the other part of her wanted to be rescued like in those fairytales.

Being reduced to a damsel in distress, though, was never in the books for Mina. She was always the rescuer, given her strength and abilities. Except for this time. Her weakness was found and used against her. The two knives in her back were no longer visible, but the blade was deep within her. She assumed that Dragos broke off the handles and threw a long coat over her to hide the evidence- and her wings- from humans while they were traveling.

The pain was becoming unbearable again and Mina could feel herself slowly succumbing to the darkness as her world went black.

****

"It seems Dragos is almost here with our dear princess," Gregor stated while sipping his late night cup of coffee.

"Yes, it does seem like I can almost sense the royal line getting closer and closer," stated Radu from across the table.

The two older men had been making preparations for the princess's arrival since they heard of Dragos' success. They had called the airline and had Dragos call them once he had boarded. From what the council had understood the princess had some secrets she had been keeping that she needed to be purged of before she could take the throne. The council trusted Dragos since the king himself had trusted him all those years ago.

"So what has Dragos said about Mina? What exactly needs purging?" asked Radu.

That was when Vasile walked into the room with a scroll rolled up in his hand, "The princess must be pure to take the throne, no flaws of any kind."

"So then we allow Dragos to do what he must for the princess?" Gregor questioned.

"Yes, if he sees something in the princess that causes her to be unworthy of the throne, allow him to do his job," replied Vasile.

The men talked amongst themselves and asked questions regarding the princess.

"The Castle construction is still underway. It should be done within the year. Although, Dragos feeding off the three night workers wasn't helpful," said Gregor.

The phone ringing brought their conversation to a halt and Gregor rose from his spot to answer the phone hanging on the wall. His conversation was brief and a lot of yes, no, perhaps. He hung the phone up and turned back to his fellow councilmen.

"Dragos has arrived. The car we sent for him is out front and the princess is in the backseat."

They all looked at each other, quietly left the dining room, and walked out the front door where they were met by the large male.

"Where is the princess?" Vasile asked.

"She is in the car, asleep. I must warn you, the way I had to go about to get her here was not pleasant and she put up a fight. I had to use some unpleasant means to get her here," Dragos replied. The three men looked confused and possibly worried about whatever tactics were used on the princess.

"What did you have to do?" Gregor questioned.

Without answering, Dragos turned and walked back towards the car and opened the backseat door. All three members gasped when they not only saw their princess, but the smell that was radiating off her.

"Have you planted your seed within her?" asked Vasile.

"I did. With her being the last pure blood female and I the last pure blood male, I expected that would be what was wanted," Dragos admitted.

"Well, preferably yes. Was it consensual?" asked Radu.

"No, but the princess has her duties. It was time she stopped playing house with that other male she had found," Dragos revealed.

"Another male? Had he laid with her as well?" said Radu.

"Yes, which is why I wasted no time in getting to the princess as I did."

Dragos shut the door and continued, "I will take her to clean her up and make sure she is presentable to you, the council, when it is time."

"We need her soon, Dragos. Especially if she could be with child," Radu replied.

"I understand. I will carry out my mission and return her to you."

With that the three men walked back into the house and Dragos got back into the vehicle. The men returned to the dining room and sat in silence, still trying to take in what they had just seen in the backseat. It was definitely their princess, but her back seemed large and she was bloodied.

"I believe I shall return to my room and pray for our princess," announced Vasile. He walked out of the room and was soon followed by the others who would do the same.

When Radu entered his room, he had a sudden urge to cry. Being a man who did not have many emotions, he feared for the princess and all she had endured. He began to pray for her safety, health, and that she was in fact being taken care of by that beast of a male.

Radu finished praying and went to his desk where many scrolls and other laws were neatly stacked like a pyramid. He began scanning the old laws when an image flashed across his mind. It was the princess in the backseat where he saw her back looked swollen. Thinking about it further he immediately rose from his seat and went downstairs to the library where they stored the much older laws and such. He scanned through multiple scrolls when he reached one that dated well before the princesses' time. It was a scroll written about her grandfather.

After reading, he discovered the lost truth of the royal bloodline. He now knew why Dragos felt the need to keep the princess away until it was time for her to take the throne. Radu knew deep within himself that he needed to find the princess before that beast did anything else to her.

Thirty Two

'This is fucking awful', Sam thought to himself. He had never flown before but he was on the last leg of his trip to Romania where he figured Mina was taken.

"Coffee? Soda?"

Sam looked up at the woman who asked him the question, "No, thank you", Sam replied. The woman smiled, looked at the person sitting beside him and asked the same question. Sam couldn't bear anymore liquids provided to him by the flight staff. He was just ready to get off the plane and be done with flying for a while. The only thing keeping him sane was repeating his plan of getting Mina over and over in his head. He knew that strength was not on his side against the male who took her, so he had to out smart him. Be quicker than him.

Staring out the small aircraft window, he thought about her. Watching the clouds pass by and thinking about her flying through them and waving at him. He almost felt himself start to smile as if he could really see her out there.

Shortly thereafter came an announcement telling them the landing routine, placing the tray tables up, put on your seatbelts, etc. Landing was by far Sam's favorite part of flying. It meant he survived the 30,000 foot high trip. Once Sam reached the airport exit, he found a cab, and was surprised that the driver actually spoke English rather well.

"Where to?" the driver asked.

"I'm going to Transylvania"

"Ah, Transylvania!" the driver said with excitement. And then held up two fingers to his front teeth and imitated a vampire.

"Yes, there." Sam tried not to roll his eyes, considering the driver didn't know he was speaking with a vampire. Oh the irony, a vampire traveling to Transylvania.

"Any specific town within Transylvania I am to take you to?" the driver asked. Sam looked at the driver with a confused look, and simply held his forefinger to the driver, "one sec" he said.

Sam pulled out his phone and looked up a map of Transylvania to decide where to start looking. He chose the town of Bran. He figured the way to hunt down the granddaughter of the infamous ruler should probably start where the lore itself lies. Bran Castle in Bran, Transylvania.

Sam gave the man his destination and the driver
opened the backseat door and closed it once Sam was
inside. They took off at an unnecessary speed and began
the journey to 'vampireland'.

The drive there was spent with the driver doing the
majority of the talking, all in english so Sam could
understand him. Telling Sam facts about the region and of
course dipping into the lore surrounding the vampire
history. After a couple hours, Sam arrived at his hotel, paid
the driver and walked inside. The hotel was nicer than Sam
was expecting, he was thinking that it would be some Inn
that was run down and run by an old man and his wife.
Nope, it was a standard hotel and had all the amenities
hotels in the U.S. had. He checked in and was given his
room key. He noticed they were setting up the dining area
for breakfast, so Sam grabbed a few items from the many
options on the buffet, then hurried to the 3rd floor and
found his room. He needed to close the blinds before the
sun came up.

Getting himself settled, he ate some of the food he
snagged from the breakfast buffet, then took a long
overdue shower. Getting a good days' sleep was necessary
for him if he was to begin his search for Mina once the sun
had set.

Before he knew it, Sam's phone alarm was going off and it was time for his night to start. He got out of bed, got dressed and grabbed his backpack.

As he walked to the elevators, he noticed a couple waiting for one to go down. He stood behind them and waited, then Sam noticed something else about them. 'Vampires,' he noted mentally. Of course there would be other vampires here of all places. Like him, they were turned, but clearly living their life just as anyone else would have. Reaching the first floor, he watched as the couple walked outside and made their way down the street.

Sam turned to go to the front desk and asked for some history. "Excuse me," Sam asked the man, "Could you tell me some of the old history about this place? Transylvania, I mean."

"Of course! We have loads of history here. Dracula is what brings most Americans here, but there is much more. Anything specific?" the man replied.

"Yes, actually, I had heard that at one point there was a royal family. Did Transylvania have a monarchy?"

"I do believe at one point there may have been one. Our history books do not state such a thing but rumors and stories have been passed down from generations."

"Ah, are there any sites I should look into? Tours?"

"Yes, a few castles would be worth visiting, one of
which is actually under restoration. There are also some
museums as well."

The man continued to tell Sam all about the many sites
to visit and also took out a map to circle the spots so he
knew where to go. Thanking the man, Sam figured he'd
start with the obvious. Bran Castle.

It was late, but Sam was about to get on the last tour,
which was classified as a ghost tour, but it got him inside.
The tour started from the bottom and worked its way
around. The guide spoke fairly decent English and told
them of the stories and some facts that could possibly back
the stories.

Yet, something caught Sam's eye. It was a large
painting of Vlad Dracul and he could see the resemblance
of his and Mina's eyes.

"Now it is said that Vlad had three sons. Two of which
unfortunately died, one from disease and the other from
battle. But, the third son lived and had a family of his own.
Legend states that the third son was also named Vlad but
he took a different last name, so he was not confused with
his father. His name was Vladimir Latislauve. It is
unknown where the last name came from or how he came
up with it. There was a nearby castle that had fallen in the
early 16th century. A portrait was found which we believe

to be him and his family. We have the portrait here, but it will be moved once that castle is restored."

The guide led the group to the portrait and Sam had to keep himself composed as he looked it over. There she was, his Mina. She was young in the picture, about the age he saw her in his dream.

Sam asked the guide, "Do you know any names of the family members?"

She replied, "I know the man is Vlad, but I'm unsure of the others," she continued, "There is an old story that stated at the fall of the castle one daughter made it out and she was never found."

Sam nodded his head like it was a cool fact, when really he was trying to keep from smiling. Knowing that he and this lost princess had been extremely intimate.

The tour concluded and everyone made their way to the gift shop while Sam made his way out to a cab and showed on the map where he would like to go. With it being night, the cab driver was reluctant at first but eventually shrugged it off and took Sam to his destination.

He decided to go to the castle that the woman from the tour talked about and just stood in awe. He had to take a moment and really look at what was before him. He thought about the fact that this is where his dear Mina grew up and where everything she talked about had happened.

Out of nowhere, a man came from the trees beside him and began speaking Romanian. Sam threw up his hands, "I don't understand you. Am I trespassing?"

"Oh you're American," the man said in English. The verbal eye roll made Sam want to tell the guy off but he let it slide.

"Yes. Sorry, but is this private property? Who are you?" Sam asked the guy.

"I'm Doru. I look after the property. Make sure no one vandalizes it or anything."

"Nice to meet you. I'm Sam. And don't worry, I'm not here to do anything bad to the place. I'm just curious about its history."

"Why are you out here at night then? That seems odd."

Sam looked the guy over and seemed confused by the question. He sensed that the guy he was talking to was another vampire. The male had medium length black hair that was pulled back except for a couple strands in the front. He had brown eyes and was about the same size as Sam. After he got a good look over the male, Sam ended up looking at him with a confused look.

"I'm just kidding, I know what you are. And I'm sure you picked up on what I am. I knew you were a fellow member of the night before I came after you. Kind of the reason I did."

273

"Oh, okay. Well, what do you know about this place? Weird question, but were you around when it was being lived in?"

"During the 16th century? Nah, I was turned in 1845. So I'm old, but I'm not that old."

"Still kinda cool, though." The two males shared information about each other and walked together towards the castle.

"Question. Have I seen you before? You look kinda familiar," Sam asked the male.

"I've been here my whole life," stated Doru.

"Huh, weird," Sam stated. But Sam could have sworn he looked just like the male from his dream. The one who showed him all those things from Mina's past.

Ignoring the deja vu, the two of them continued to the castle.

More Romanian words were shouted from out of nowhere, which Sam was easily able to figure out were directed at them.

What appeared to be a security guard and Daru spoke a few words and then the security guard walked off with no protest.

"What did you say to him?" Sam asked.

"I told him I take care of the grounds and that I have permission from the family to be here."

"Why does that not sound like the truth?"

"Well, I do take care of the grounds, but the family who owns it? I have no idea who that is."

They continued walking around the castle and Sam tried to imagine the castle as it was back in its prime.

Sam came to an abrupt halt and grabbed Daru by the arm, pulling him down to the castle wall.

"What was that for?" Daru demanded.

"Trust me, just be quiet," Sam requested.

Thirty Three

Mina awoke to find herself in a cold, dark, wet place. She was laying on a dirt floor with her hands bound by metal cuffs. Fully opening her eyes, she sat up and noticed that the pain in her back was not as severe as it was on her trip to wherever she was.

She breathed in the air and couldn't place where she was. She tried her best to stand, but could not find the strength needed to get her legs to work. Instead, she pushed herself up against the cold stone wall and just sat there. There was a lantern lit at her, 'Am I in a cell?' she asked mentally.

Something about the place seemed familiar but she couldn't place it. Her senses were thrown off due to the pain and not feeding in who knows how long at this point.

Mina knew to stay silent. She needed as much time as possible to think. She didn't call out to see if anyone else was there, she just sat with her thoughts. That's when she heard what sounded like a wooden door opening. Loud heavy footsteps were approaching her, which immediately told her who it was.

"Well, hello princess. So nice of you to awaken finally," Dragos said.

"Where am I?"

"Do you not know? Come on, you're smarter than that."

Mina looked again and nothing seemed familiar, "Well, you could get me something to feed from and then I could figure it out," she replied.

"You think I'm a fool? You will be fed when I allow you to be fed. Shall I help you out then? I'll give you a hint. I spent a lot of time here when you were a young girl."

Mina felt her heart skip as she finally realised why the place had seemed familiar. He had brought her back to her home, but to the dungeon.

"How is this still here?" she asked.

"It's underground and the fire never reached the lower levels. Seriously, girl, I was told you were smart," Dragos said, making Mina seem ignorant.

"What do you want from me?"

"Well, I don't need you. The council does. And they know about what happened in Georgia. They are pleased I took you and planted myself inside you."

Mina shivered as she remembered that night when he took her. A slight wince flashed across her face, which Dragos noticed.

"Don't act like you didn't enjoy it. I know you tried to fake it because you didn't want to make that male feel bad, but I could tell you wanted more."

"You tell that to all of your females?"

Ignoring her question, he began to use his right hand to rub himself, as if to become hard and come at her for round two. Mina was ready to fight him even though her legs wouldn't work. He was about to unlock her cell when he stopped and turned his head to the side as if he was listening for something.

"I'll be back for you," Dragos stated. With that, he left her alone again and she tried like hell to get her legs to move. No luck. She had to figure something out before he came back.

****

"What are you doing?" asked Doru.

"Will you shut up? Just trust me," replied Sam quietly.

Sam watched as that large male who took Mina walked up out of a door that was laid in the ground. He knew the male was older and could possibly hear Sam and

Daru with no problem. Sam looked at his new acquaintance and hinted that they should get out of there as quickly and quietly as possible. Daru nodded back in agreement and the two of them bolted in the opposite direction. Sam looked behind him once they were a fair distance away and saw that the male had gone over to the spot where he and Daru were just at.

"Who is that?" questioned Doru.

"I'm not sure of his name, but I do know he is much older than you. He is actually part of the real reason I'm here."

"And?" Daru asked with impatience.

"There is this female. She apparently used to live here. I was with her in the States and he came to where we were living and took her."

The look Sam witnessed on Doru's face was that of 'holy shit'.

"What?" Sam asked.

"What is her name? If she is from here, perhaps I may know her."

"Her name is Wilhelmina. Wilhelmina Latislauve."

Daru looked at Sam with a blank expression and Sam began to wonder what was going through this guy's mind. It wasn't a moment later that Daru spoke up, "Like, as in, the lost princess?"

"I suppose so. You know the story?"

"Yeah, I've heard people in the small village near here talk about it in some of the bars."

The two of them exchanged looks and then looked back at the castle.

"If that guy is as old as this place, then we may be in some serious trouble."

"Oh, well I'm not sure how old he is, but Mina is old and he knew her. Knew her well actually," Sam stated.

"Well, I'm here to help in any way I can," said Doru.

"Thanks. I believe I'm going to need all the help I can get."

The pair stayed put for an hour or so, just watching the castle.

When out of nowhere, they both heard a scream coming from the castle. A female scream.

Sam began running towards the castle, but did not get far before Daru tackled him to the ground and pinned him down. His primal male side began kicking in but Daru was strong and kept Sam in his place.

"Get off me!" Sam demanded.

"No, you need to be careful and not just go in there with no plan."

"I have a plan! I'm going to rip that fucker's head off!"

The wrestling continued for a moment and then Sam succumbed to his defeat.

"I know you hear her, but we have to play this smart. You can't help her if you're dead, too."

Daru removed himself from Sam and helped him to his feet. They retreated back to the tree line.

"The time will come for you to make your move. And, if this female is as strong as you say she is, then she won't go without a fight. Now follow me. You can stay with me and we can figure out a plan. Tomorrow night, we will go get her."

Sam agreed and followed Daru to his place.

The two males arrived at a small, run down cottage that could more accurately be referred to as a shack. It was surrounded by dead plants and what appeared to be an abandoned car.

"This is where you live?" Sam asked.

"It's not much, but it's a roof over my head."

"Fair."

They walked through the front door and sat at what Daru called a table, which was mostly just a couple chairs and a large wooden crate. Daru brought over a couple glasses and poured a dark red substance from a container. The iron smell hit his nose and his fangs tingled with need. He drank the glass so quickly, it was only a second he asked for more.

"I don't have much and we need this for tomorrow," Daru said.

Sam didn't care. Any amount would work. But then he felt what was usually a welcome feeling, but was highly unwanted right now. When he was with Mina, they always fucked after feeding, due to the hightened emotions. Now? He was alone with another male, the thought of which caused Sam to think to himself, 'No fucking way'.

"You okay?" Daru asked.

"Um, yeah, do you have a bathroom?" Sam questioned. He didn't see any other room, but he needed a place to take care of himself.

"I don't. Typically I just go to the woods, as if I was camping."

"Oh. um, okay." Sam looked at Daru and, as if they spoke without saying words, Daru said, "I see. I get it. When I first started feeding that happened to me, too. I'll go out and hunt for a while. You do what you need and I'll be back before sunrise."

No other words were exchanged. Males understood male problems.

And, just like that, Sam was alone.

"How the fuck am I able to do this right now? Mina is probably being tortured and I'm over here with a hard on," Sam said into the empty space.

Sam paced for a minute, and the thing still hadn't gone away. He had to give himself a release and just move on. He sat back down in the chair and unbuttoned his pants so he could access what he needed. He quickly slid his hand down his pants and took hold of what was protruding underneath.

He gasped as he held himself and began stroking slowly at first, then picked up the pace. His breathing became labored and he could feel himself getting closer and closer to his needed release. At the last minute, Sam grabbed a napkin off the table and came hard into it. He threw his head back from the pleasure and bit his lip with enough force to make it bleed. He continued to breathe hard and used the napkin to clean himself up, then threw it away in the trash. He felt disgusting for doing that when he needed to try and rescue his female, but it was too close to dawn for him to do anything now. He could only hope that his female was strong enough to not give up and hold out for him to get to her.

Thirty Four

When Dragos returned to Mina, he forced himself upon her not once or twice, but three times. She tried to fight him off, but she just didn't have the energy or the strength to be successful. She had never felt so helpless as she did in that moment. All those years she spent without a man violating her, to come down to this one moment where she could not fight back or protect herself.

After the third time, Dragos left her laying on the cold ground like a piece of trash. She could feel herself wanting to cry, but held back her tears. She may be weak at that moment, but she refused to let him see her pain.

It was an hour or so before Dragos returned to her and said, "Now princess, let's get you fixed up."

Mina could hear chains dragging on the ground as he came closer to her. He picked her up by her neck and ripped off her remaining clothes, then bound her up. She was fully exposed, but at this point she didn't care.

He grabbed her by her cuffs and mercilessly dragged her out of her cell, then lifted her up onto a table. The cold metal against her bare skin made her wince but it was nothing compared to the pain from within. He lifted up some kind of tool looking thing and walked to the end of the table.

"What…. What are you going to do?" she asked, suddenly unable to breathe.

"I told you, I'm going to fix you. A creature such as yourself should not bear children who could one day rule."

"What? The council, they want this?"

"What they don't know won't hurt them."

Mina let out a scream, as loud as she could. She used every last bit of strength she had to kick her somewhat lifeless legs and make it difficult for him to gain access. He grabbed her by the knees and tried his best to open her legs, but instead landed a good blow to her lower abdomen.

Mina felt all the air in her lungs escape her as he planted his knife into her. Her head fell backwards and she felt her legs being lifted and he exposed her once again. She felt something sharp enter her and all the pain she had felt up until now was nothing compared to what he was doing to her at that moment.

Dragos never had any medical training, so what he was doing was just mutilating whatever he could feel with his knife. She felt the blood running down her leg and under her. Then, the sharp tool was removed and she felt as if her insides could fall out of her at any point. If she didn't feed soon, there would be no recovery from this.

"Good girl, now just one more thing." Dragos laid the bloodied tool down and walked up next to her. He looked down at her and said "I'm going to send you where you have belonged this entire time. You will suffer and die alone just like your dear Dimitri did."

That was when Mina sat up quickly and head butted the bastard right in the face as hard as she could. She slammed back down onto the table, nose bleeding, and Dragos was holding his nose as it had most likely had broken. The anger in his eyes made her happy because she knew she got one good blow to him before he killed her.

In a split second, she was flipped from her back to her stomach and she realised what he was about to do.

Mina felt as though her screams would never end, but then her world became black and she accepted the fact that she had died.

****

Daru returned with more blood and Sam looked over at him, almost embarrassed at what he had just done.

"Listen, I told you I get it. There is no need to be weird about it," Daru said. This made Sam feel a little better about the situation. The two of them sat down at the table and discussed possible plan ideas and what would work or wouldn't work.

"Listen, the south side of the castle would be best. We can enter where the old stable was. There is a hidden passage there that would get us in and out," Daru mentioned.

"That would probably work. Wait, how do you know that?" Sam questioned.

"I, um, I've been around the property a lot and I've explored things."

"Yeah? Okay."

"Anyway, I think that would be perfect. That way we don't have to use the same entrance as him. Dragos is very smart, given his…" Daru trailed off as Sam stared at him.

"Dragos? Is that his name? Seriously, how would you know that?" Sam questioned. His face was stern. He needed to know who Daru really was.

"I saw a picture of him in some old paintings, I swear." Daru was trying a little too hard to make Sam believe him.

"I don't believe you. I-" Sam was cut off and both whipped their heads towards the back wall of the house. Looking back at each other, they smelled a large amount of blood.

"What would that be? Hunters?" Sam asked.

"I doubt it. There aren't a lot of hunters around here. This is still a part of the castle grounds."

They rose out of their chairs and were about to exit the door when they stopped. The sun had risen and neither of them could leave. Sam had a feeling in the pit of his stomach that he needed to see why there was a sudden large amount of blood smell, but he couldn't do anything about it with the sun out.

The pair returned to the chairs at the table and sat down.

"Well, we have nothing else to do. Might as well tell me your real past."

Daru seemed hesitant to talk about it, but eventually gave in. "Fine, I wasn't turned in 1845. I was turned in 1503 and then a year later sold to the king as a servant boy. I cleaned around the castle while the family slept during the day."

Sam sat in shock from what he was hearing, "So you knew Mina?"

"I knew of her, I only saw her every so often. Never talked to her," Daru answered.

"So the fires, or attacks. How did you survive?"

"I was tasked with collecting meat in town for the king's dinner. I heard the commotion and rushed back, but everything was up in flames."

Sam sat back in his chair, "So all this time, you knew more about the guy and you just let me think you had no idea."

"I understand you're upset. I get it. But, we need to continue working together if we are going to get the princess away from Dragos."

They both sat quietly for a while and then continued on with their plans for rescue.

8 hours later....

Sam and Daru were standing at the door, waiting for the sun to get below the horizon so they could make their move towards the scent of blood. Once the sky darkened they bolted out from the little house and tracked the scent of iron across a field and into the woods near the castle.

"It has to be around here somewhere, the smell is strongest right in this area," Sam said, as he looked around trying to find whatever it was they were looking for.

He took a few more steps forward and then he heard a faint heartbeat with extremely shallow breathing. Somehow he knew that he needed to get to whoever that was. He began to run and didn't think twice about where Daru had ended up.

All the blood in Sam's body ran cold the moment he saw her body. He froze with fear but soon rushed over to her. It was his Mina.

"Mina! Baby, can you hear me? Wake up!" Sam screamed in desperation, trying to get her to open her eyes or even move a limb. Yet, she didn't move and didn't speak, and her eyes didn't open.

She had been laying on the cold forest floor all day, exposed to a small amount of sunlight, naked. Sam looked over her body and he was stunned by what he saw. She had been bleeding from her face, back, stomach, and… "Oh god, no." he said as he looked at the dried blood between her legs.

He gathered her in his arms and just held her, assuming it wouldn't be long before she was going to pass. It was at that moment he wanted to trade his own life for hers, take away her pain and help her get out of this mess.

As he was cradling his female, Daru came up to him and Sam got protective. His eyes became dark and his fangs fully extended, warning Daru to keep his distance.

"Easy, Sam, I'm not going to touch her. But, we need to get her back to my place so you can feed her and take care of her."

It took Sam a minute to come down from his male instincts, and agree with what Daru said. He stood up, with Mina still in his arms, and walked back to the little house.

Once they arrived, Sam placed Mina on the poor excuse of a bed and covered her up with a blanket. Daru brought over the blood and handed it to Sam. Sam appreciated that his friend had respect for him to be the one to feed her.

Sam opened the jar and used his finger to run some blood on the inside of Mina's mouth. Once he did that, he could hear her heart slowly begin to return to its usual rhythm. He provided her with a little more, being careful not to drown her. Soon he could see her wounds begin to close and her skin was less pale. Yet, she still was not waking up.

"It's going to take some time, Sam. Give it an hour and then give her some more. I'll make sure we have plenty of blood on hand for when she wakes up," Daru said.

Sam nodded, but his eyes never left Mina. He watched her chest rise and fall as she inhaled and exhaled. Waiting for the moment her eyes open and she sees that he is there, in Romania, for her.

He held her hand in his and dropped his lips down to kiss it. Her cold hand was as lifeless as she seemed, but he knew the more blood she ingested, the more she would heal.

Taking initiative, Sam rose from his seat and got some water to clean her up. Daru had left to get more blood, from wherever that may be, and he took advantage of the time he had alone with his female.

He began by running the wet cloth across her cheeks and around her nose. Then he moved to her ribs where a small hole sat, but was almost closed. He fully removed the blanket so he could see all of her, only looking for additional wounds he could clean up. He found the one at her lower abdomen.

He never studied anatomy, but he could easily guess that's where her womb would lie. "That bastard," said Sam, as he gently wiped the blood away, so all that was left was the open wound.

He moved to the part he dreaded most, the blood that was between her legs. He was gentle with every move he made. He opened her legs and continued cleaning up the horrific aftermath or what that asshole put her through. He could tell something sharp was placed into her, based on the amount of blood that stained her skin, but he didn't know enough to examine her. He finished cleaning her, closed her legs and placed the blanket back over her to keep her warm.

He was about to place the cloth in the bucket and be done, until he remembered her back had also been bleeding when he found her. Preparing himself, he carefully rolled her to her side and saw the real damage that beast did.

There, where her wings used to sit, was nothing but sawed off bone and blood.

Sam broke for her, his tears flooded his eyes as he took the cloth once again and cleaned the blood that covered her back. He would take a moment to wipe his eyes, and then return to cleaning her. Once he was done, he moved her onto her back and made sure she was fully covered. He dumped the bloody water and rang the cloth out.

Returning to his female, still with tears in his eyes, he took her hand and spoke, "My Mina. My sweet, strong, beautiful Mina. I am so sorry I couldn't be there to save you from this. I will be here when you wake, and never leave your side. Even if it kills me. I love you."

He kissed her hand once more and then fed her more blood. This time, her lips formed around the rim of the jar and she drank it herself. She didn't drink much before she laid back down again, but he watched as more life came back to her. He sat with her the whole time, not moving from his spot for anything.

Thirty Five

Mina could hear sounds in the distance but could not tell who or what they were. Voices maybe? She felt like she could move, yet could tell that her limbs were not moving as she commanded. Then, she heard, "I love you."

'Sam?' she asked mentally, 'Was Sam here? With her? Was he dead as well?'

Her mind began to race with many questions and it made her want to open her eyes even more. She needed to see her male. The sweet taste of blood entered her mouth every so often which made her feel more and more alive. 'How would I feel alive if I know I died in that dungeon?' she questioned. She could hear another male voice but couldn't place it. She drifted off once more, and began to watch her life as if it was an interactive movie.

"Wilhelmina, my dear, come talk to me," came a female voice from behind her. Mina turned around and saw a woman with a white dress sitting on a bench.

"Mother?" she asked.

"Yes, my dear. Come and talk with me. Tell me of the life you have lived after I left."

Mina told her mother everything that she went through, through the many decades and centuries, the ups and the downs. She told her about Sam and the hope to one day have children and be married. She unloaded everything and began to cry as she told her mother the horrible thing Dragos did to her in the field.

"My dear, you are so brave and strong. Your father and I are so proud of you and who you have become."

"Is father here?"

"He is not, but I know for a fact he is proud."

Mina was crying her eyes out at this point, and her mother pulled her in and let Mina cry on her shoulder.

"It is okay, my dear, you let it out. You deserve to let your emotions out like this. You can't be the strong warrior forever."

Mina pulled away and looked at her mother. No words were exchanged, yet a lot was said. Mina felt peace for the first time since she had been taken from Sam and asked her mother, "Am I dead?"

Her mother let out a slight giggle and said, "No, my love, you are not. You did come close, but no. You have some people who truly care for you and who are taking care of you now. I must make one request, though."

"Yes?"

"Be sure to live your life without fear of what is to come. Love without boundaries and open your heart to whatever or whomever enters your life. I know you can be stubborn and love your freedom, but I do enjoy watching you smile. That's it! I request you smile more, my dear."

"I will, mother. I promise."

With that her mother placed her hand upon Mina's face, stared at her daughter for a moment, then stood up from the bench and walked away.

"Mother?" Mina called out.

Her mother returned shortly after her departure, holding something in her arms that was small and wrapped in a blanket.

As she came closer, Mina realised that what she was holding was a baby.

"Who is this?" Mina asked.

"This is what was supposed to be. That which two people in love had created. Yet, taken before a heartbeat could have been heard."

Mina felt her eyes begin to sting and she looked up to her mothers eyes with pain.

"Is this..... mine?" Mina questioned.

Her mother had no answer, just stood while Mina continued to gaze upon the young in her arms. Something in her heart made her feel sadness but peace as well, knowing this child would be with her mother.

Then, as if being pulled from behind, she was lifted out of her white paradise and into darkness.

****

Four days had passed since Sam found Mina in the woods. He had been slowly feeding her every 30 minutes until she only needed blood every 2 hours. It was 12am and Sam felt her stir in the bed. He took her hand and squeezed it while reassuring her that she wasn't alone and that she was safe. Mina settled and as if it was the moment to happen, Mina slowly lifted her eyelids.

"Doru!" Sam shouted

Daru came running over to the bedside, but stayed behind Sam out of respect.

Her voice was hoarse but she spoke, "Where.... Where am I?"

"You are here at my friend's house. Doru, he used to work at your home all those years ago."

Mina glanced at Sam and then over to the other male. Sam watched as her eyes widened.

"Mina? What's wrong? Are you okay?" Sam asked his female

Sam soon realized that she was looking at Doru.

"Mina, what is it?"

That's when she spoke, clear as day, "Dimitri?"

Follow for more!

Updates and sneak peaks posted

weekly!

Facebook.com/HeirofShadows

Book 2....
2026!